"You're lucky to have such a good friend."

Tracy looked up at the faintly wistful tone in David's voice. "Are you getting to know a few people?"

"Some. It takes time in a small town. I should learn to play golf. Apparently that helps."

"You might want to start small."

He winked at her. "Getting there. I'm working on my minigolf game, but the dreaded windmill still eludes me."

"Many a good man has been tripped up on that one," she said, his gentle teasing drawing an answering smile.

He held her gaze, a sense of expectation hovering between them. Then he disappeared into his office.

Voices old and new reminded her. *Be careful. Guard your heart. No one else is going to take care of you.*

But as she slipped on her sweater and caught her purse, she felt as if she was warning herself more out of habit than conviction.

Books by Carolyne Aarsen

Love Inspired

*Stealing Home

CAROLYNE AARSEN

and her husband, Richard, live on a small ranch in northern Alberta, where they have raised four children and numerous foster children, and are still raising cattle. Carolyne crafts her stories in her office with a large west-facing window through which she can watch the changing seasons while struggling to make her words obey.

A SILENCE
IN THE HEART

CAROLYNE AARSEN

Steeple
Hill®

Published by Steeple Hill Books™

STEEPLE HILL BOOKS

Steeple Hill®

ISBN 0-373-87327-1

A SILENCE IN THE HEART

www.SteepleHill.com

Printed in U.S.A.

But as for me, I watch in hope for the Lord,
I wait for God my Savior; my God will hear me.
—*Micah* 7:7

For Justin, our most precious foster child.
Our time with you was too short.

For his able and interesting advice on
all things concerning animals and veterinarians,
I'd like to thank Dr. Ed Doornenbal.

Chapter One

She thought she heard the cry of a child.

The haunting sound slid through the early-morning quiet just as Tracy stepped out of her car. Still holding the door, she canted her head to one side, listening.

There it was again. Softer this time.

Tracy strode around the concrete-block building trying to pinpoint the origin. But when she came around the side of the building, the street in front of the clinic was empty as well.

The tension in her shoulders loosened and she shivered, pulling her thin sweater closer around herself. Ever the optimist, she had left her warmer jacket hanging in the hallway closet of her apartment this morning, counting on the early-September sun to melt away the coolness of the fall morning.

A movement caught her eye.

She stopped and watched a small boy shuffle cautiously around the corner of the clinic, his head angled down, his thin arms cradling something. He looked to be about six or seven.

Tracy recognized him. For the past two weeks he had walked past the clinic in the early morning on his way to school. The last few days he had stopped to look in the window. It had taken a few encouraging waves and smiles to tease one from his wary face.

Tracy might have been inadequately dressed for the weather, but the boy was even more so. He wore a short-sleeved T-shirt, faded blue jeans and sandals on bare feet. As she watched, he shivered lightly.

"Hey, there," Tracy said quietly, not wanting to startle him.

"I want to see the doctor," he said, sniffing lightly as Tracy came nearer. "This kitten got hurt." He angled a suspicious glance through the tangle of dark hair hanging in his brown eyes.

"The veterinarian isn't in yet." Tracy crouched down. The tiny ball of mangled fur tucked in his arms looked to be in rough shape.

One eye was completely closed, the fur around it matted with blood. A leg hung at an awkward angle. Probably broken.

"What happened?" she asked quietly.

"I dunno. I just found him laying here." The little boy stood stiffly, his body language defensive. "Can you fix him?"

Tracy's heart sank. She knew the little boy couldn't pay the vet fees, doubted his parents could.

"I wanna keep him," the little boy wiped his nose on

the shoulder of his T-shirt, a hitch in his voice. "He can be my friend."

Tracy's thoughts jumped to herself, age eight, standing in the kitchen of the apartment she and her mother shared, saying the same words, also holding a kitten.

"Not enough money," her mother had said, though Velma managed to magically find it for other things. How Tracy had longed for that kitten. A friend.

Tracy pushed herself to her feet. "Let's go inside."

The boy slanted her a narrow-eyed, wary look, holding back as she unlocked the door and opened it.

"It's okay," Tracy said quietly. "We have to go inside to look at your kitten."

He nodded and slowly stepped inside, his head swiveling around, checking out the reception area of the clinic.

"What's your name?" she asked as the door fell shut behind them.

"Are you a stranger?" he asked, suspicion edging his voice. "My mom says I'm not s'posed to talk to strangers."

"I'm a vet technician," she answered, sidestepping the guarded question. "And my name is Tracy Harris."

He stood in the center of the room, a tightly wound bundle of vigilance, clinging to the kitten like a lifeline. His eyes darted around—assessing, watchful. They met Tracy's as he straightened, as if making a decision. "My name is Kent," he said with a quick lift of his chin. "Kent Cordell."

She had been given a small gift of trust and in spite of the kitten that might be dying in his arms, she gave Kent a smile. She skimmed his shoulder with her fingers. "Good to meet you, Kent."

The back door slammed and a loud singing broke the quiet. Crystal, the other vet technician burst into the room with her usual dramatic flair. "And a good morning to you, my dear," she called out, then stopped when she saw Kent.

Kent tucked his head over the kitten, his shoulders hunched in defense. Like a turtle he had withdrawn again.

Crystal angled her chin at Kent. "Who's the kid?"

"This is Kent, and I'm bringing him and his kitten to an examining room. As soon as Dr. Harvey comes in, can you send him my way?"

"Not Dr. Braun?" Crystal asked with a faint smirk.

Tracy was disappointed at the faint blush warming her neck. From the first day that David had started at the clinic four months ago, Crystal had been avidly watching the two of them, as if it was only a matter of time before they started dating. As a result Tracy always felt extra self-conscious around David—which in turn annoyed her. She had learned her own lessons about men and their lack of faithfulness. She didn't need to have the lesson underlined with yet another man.

"Just send Dr. Harvey in when he comes."

Crystal pouted. "Okay, okay I'll just be in the supply room." She swung around, her lab coat flaring out behind her as she strode down the hall.

David Braun glanced at the clock on the dashboard of his truck as he pulled up beside Tracy's rusted sports car. Seven-thirty. He had planned on beating her here this morning and showing that he could be as punctual and time-conscious as she was.

Guess I'll have to put off the good impression until tomorrow, he thought as he stepped out of the truck, taking a moment to look around.

The chill morning air held the scent of fall. Moldering leaves, grain dust from the harvest and the acrid scent of burning.

Below him, nestled in the valley of the Paddle River, lay the town of Preston, the houses guarded by smooth-barked aspen trees, their golden and orange leaves illuminating the morning. The changing of the season brought a touch of melancholy tinged with guilt. In a couple of weeks Heather's family would be convening in the nearby town of Kolvik for the first anniversary of her death. He owed it to the family to take part, even though he had moved on from that sad place.

Through the last months of Heather's life, David had gone through the motions of a relationship that had faded away well before her diagnosis of cancer. He had been trying to find a way to break up with her when she got the news. So he had stayed at her side, and when she'd died, he had felt a guilty sense of freedom.

Then he'd moved here and met Tracy. Cute, spunky and willful.

He was still trying to figure out why he was even remotely attracted to her. She wasn't his type at all.

Even so, as he pushed open the back door and walked down the hallway, he couldn't stop a flicker of anticipation at seeing her again.

"Bright and early. That's my boy."

David spun around. Crystal stood in the doorway, her arms crossed over a lab coat. "Glad you came in early.

Tracy's in one of the treatment rooms with a kitten and a kid."

"A kitten? Already?"

"Some people never rest." Crystal waved him on with a wink. "Go and impress her with my blessing." And before he could protest, she was gone.

David followed the sound of Tracy's voice.

"We'll just lay it down here now, okay?"

David heard a murmured response.

He paused in the doorway of one of the treatment rooms. Tracy stood in profile to him, her eyes intent on a small kitten slumped on the stainless-steel table, her dark eyebrows pulled together in a frown. Across from her, a little boy stood on a stool looking as attentively as she at the animal.

Tracy, with her short dark hair like a cap framing her delicate features. The little boy with his long hair hanging past his eyes. They could almost be sister and brother. Not that he would know. All he'd ever found out from her was a brief mention of her mother, who seemed to be no more.

Tracy glanced sideways, as if sensing his presence and straightened when she saw him. "David. I'm so glad you're here. This kitten. It's not…" She stopped, angling a quick look at the little boy who had backed quickly into a corner of the room. "Please. Have a look at it."

He was momentarily taken aback by her muddled words and by the boy's defensive posture. Tracy's fine veneer of reserve had been both a challenge and a barrier when he'd first met her.

"Please," she asked, stepping toward him, her one hand lifted as if in supplication.

"What's wrong?" He ventured a smile and was rewarded with a surprising lift of her lips that did funny things to his heart.

"The left Achilles tendon is severed," she told him, all business now as she stepped aside for him.

David gently palpated the abdomen, lifted the back leg, pushing aside the matted fur to check. "Any blood work done yet?" David murmured, lifting an eyelid.

"Not yet."

David glanced at the little boy who was staring at him, his expression guarded and wary.

"This is Kent," Tracy said, her expression softening as she looked down at the little boy. She looked almost maternal.

"Hi, there, Kent. I'm Dr. Braun," David said with a smile.

Kent just nodded and looked down.

"We'll see what we can do." David straightened. "He'll have to wait outside, though."

Kent looked back at the kitten and David caught a fleeting glimpse of pain.

Tracy laid her hand on his shoulder. "It will be okay, Kent. Dr. Braun can fix your kitty." Tracy glanced up at David, her eyebrows raised in question.

David shrugged one shoulder in a vague gesture.

Tracy ushered the reluctant boy out of the room, speaking to him in a low, encouraging voice. He didn't look as if he was buying her assurances, but he went along anyway.

David turned back to the kitten. It was so small, its skin so fragile. It would require a delicate hand. And even then…

"I've got him settled. For now." Tracy closed the door behind her, leaning against it, her dark eyes intent on his. "What's the prognosis?"

"I won't know for sure until we get the X-rays back. But for now, I see it's going to take a fair bit of work. I don't know if it's worth it."

"I'll pay for it." Her voice was firm.

"What I'm saying is that it might die in spite of what I'm going to do," he said quietly.

She tugged on her lip, wavering. "But you'll do it."

David looked at the kitten, still hesitating. The cost was going to be high. The chances slim. Why did this matter to her? "Is the boy a relative?"

"No. I found him at the front of the clinic holding the kitten."

He nodded, giving her a puzzled glance. "So why are you willing to do this?"

"Because it matters to him." The decisive note in her voice told him that was all he was going to get for now.

"It sounds like it matters to you, too," David said gently.

She relaxed at that, gave him another smile, more open than the first and David felt that funny little flip again. "It does."

"Then let's get going."

"Heart is still steady, thankfully," Tracy said to David, unhooking the stethoscope from her ears. "I don't think I can go much lower on the anaesthetic."

She adjusted the cone over the kitten's mouth and nose and tightened the band behind its ears.

"So far so good, little guy," she whispered, adjusting the surgical drapes over its tiny body. Beyond the door, she heard Crystal chatting with Kent, although the conversation sounded mostly one sided. She had tried to convince him to let Crystal take him to school but he adamantly refused to leave.

"Grab the clamps, please."

Tracy reached under David's hands, holding pressure on the handles that held the tendon. The kitten was so small, they had to work closely. Tracy caught a whiff of his aftershave as he stitched, a pleasantly distracting scent that overrode the pervasive scent of old plastic that came from the vaporizer.

He turned his head and for a flash, their eyes met.

Tracy looked hastily down, surprised at her frisson of awareness. Okay, so he was good-looking, if your tastes ran to tousled blond hair and deep-set eyes. So he was, well, nice.

A dull word, that didn't explain the appeal that was alternately confusing and frightening. Art had taught her hard enough lessons on the value of keeping herself unattached, but guarding her heart was becoming tough to do around David. She didn't like it, but didn't know how to change it other than to quit. Which she'd never do. Working with animals was her sanctuary. They never let you down. Never broke your heart.

"Hold the leg, please," David murmured pulling a prethreaded needle from a plastic case. His large hands danced in intricate movements as he spun the suture thread around the forceps, tying off, each movement precise and sure. He was good at what he did. Quicker and more confident than Dr. Harvey. So far they had only been at work for an hour and a quarter and they were almost done.

"Cut the ends long," David said as he straightened. "You don't want to be digging around too much to get the stitches out."

"You do good work," Tracy said quietly, swabbing the area once more.

"Thanks."

"You sound surprised." Tracy glanced up at him, puzzled by the tone of his voice.

A crooked smile lifted one corner of his mouth, creasing one cheek. "You're not one for lots of compliments. That's all."

He picked up the assorted forceps and scissors, dropping them into the metal tray with a clang and stripping off the surgical gloves.

"Well, I appreciate the time you took to work on this kitten."

"Do you know this little boy?"

"I've seen him off and on going past the office." Tracy untied the mask and eased it off the kitten's head. "This morning was the first time I talked to him. I don't know if he even owns the kitten."

"A stray?"

"I think so. But like I said, I'll pay for it."

"It's not a problem, Tracy," David said stroking one large finger down the side of the kitten's head. He looked up at her, still smiling.

And Tracy felt that dangerous yearning once again. The moment was broken by the click of the door opening and Alan Harvey entered the room. "My two favorite people, hard at work already. Crystal said you had a badly injured kitten. Need any help?"

"Just finished," David said tossing the latex gloves into the garbage can in the corner. "Broken pelvis and a severed Achilles tendon."

"Looks like everything here is under control." Alan Harvey brushed his thinning hair back over his head, adjusted his pants over his broad stomach as if preparing for a hard day's work. "So, Tracy, what's on tap for me today?"

"You've got a herd health appointment at the Hutterite colony, Lana Andrews wants you to declaw her cats and Steenbergens need some preg testing done." Tracy leveled a warning frown at him as she wrapped the discarded tools in the used surgical drapes. "So no pie and coffee with Frank and Matilda at the colony, no chitchat with the other customers. You get behind, you get stressed, and you know what your own doctor said about that."

Alan just laughed. "Does she boss you around like this, David?"

"Not yet." David's glance caught hers, a light of challenge in their hazel depths. "But I'm sure that can change."

Tracy felt it again. The subtle question that drifted between them, like a whispered invitation.

She held his gaze a moment, as if testing her resolve. Then, out of the corner of her eye she caught Alan Harvey's intent look—and the grin splitting his face.

"I'll take the kitten away now," she said, willing the warmth creeping up her neck to go away.

David and Alan left, discussing the work of the day, giving Tracy a few moments to compose herself.

"Here's our little man," Crystal said, returning with Kent. She gave Tracy a warning look. "And he's not very happy with me."

"Thanks, Crystal."

Kent, still glowering, walked slowly up to Tracy.

"You can come with me to put the kitten in the kennel," Tracy said by way of a peace offering. He only nodded, following her.

She slowed her steps to match Kent's: he was looking vigilantly around, like a little prisoner checking out escape routes. His behavior raised questions that, for now, Tracy kept to herself. She was thankful he was at least willing to be with her.

For now all she could do was try to earn his trust. And she sensed the kitten was the bridge to the little boy.

She settled the kitten in the cage, turning him so his head was in the front. "There. He'll be a little sleepy for a while, but when he wakes up we'll give him some food."

Kent nodded once, apparently satisfied with her explanation. Tracy ushered him out the door and closed it carefully behind them.

"So what do you think your mom will say about the kitten?" Tracy asked, fishing lightly for information as they walked back to the reception area.

Kent dropped his head. "I dunno."

"Do you think she'll let you keep him?"

His lack of response sent regret twanging through Tracy. She knew the cost of the work David had just done. The aftercare cost. If Kent didn't take the kitten, she was stuck with trying to find a home for an expensive mongrel. Her landlord had a strict no-pets rule. But if it made this boy smile, if it would make him happy, it was a chance worth taking.

"Well, you'd better get home before she misses you," Tracy said with false heartiness.

Kent lifted one thin shoulder in a vague shrug and Tracy's regret was replaced by disquiet.

"Is your mother home?" Tracy asked, careful to keep her tone neutral.

A quick nod.

She hesitated over the next question but asked anyhow. "And your dad?"

"I don't have a dad." Kent clutched a fraying string at his neck.

Tracy caught the familiar movement. She suspected the string he clung to held the key to his home. His fragile lifeline.

Unwanted memories flashed through her head. Moments of blinding, numbing panic when she couldn't find the string of her own key to her apartment. Then the flood of relief when the key was discovered either tucked absently into a pants pocket or one time when the string had been caught on a button of her coat.

Tracy glanced at her watch. Nine-thirty. "I think we should get you to school now."

He was already late. But when Crystal had brought up bringing him he got so upset about leaving his kitten, Tracy had been called out of surgery to settle him down. They decided Tracy would bring him when she could.

"I'm ready," Kent answered with a frown. "I just hafta walk there."

"All by yourself?"

"Yeah." Kent tossed the word out as if questioning her intelligence.

Tracy took a calming breath. This little guy could barely reach the crossing-light button on Main Street, never mind negotiate the streets of Preston in the fall. Logging trucks just beginning their season and grain trucks bringing the harvest into the grain terminal would be thundering down the street. And it didn't look as if he had a lunch either.

She bit her lip, calculating whether she had time to help him out. Mr. Stinson had promised to call her this morning. He was so unpredictable, no telling what would happen if she wasn't here to take his call.

But she couldn't let this little fellow head out on his own. She walked over to Crystal's desk and wrote a quick note to her about what to do should Edgar Stinson call while she was gone.

"Tracy, can you tell me where I can find some more latex gloves?" David stood in the doorway of the room, a pair of coveralls over one arm. "Crystal didn't know."

"I'll get them for you and then I'm going to take Kent to school." She paused, then added, "If that's okay." Dr. Harvey would have sent her on her way with a wave of his hand, but she still had to find her way around the new territory that was David Braun.

In more ways than one.

David held her steady gaze. "Probably a good idea."

His approbation kindled a glimmer of warmth. "I'll be back in about twenty minutes," she said, glancing down at Kent. "I think I'll take him home so he can put on some clean clothes."

Kent frowned. "I put this on yesterday."

"Carrying that kitten made your shirt all dirty," David said, planting one large finger on a spot on Kent's chest.

Kent jerked back, slapping David's hand away. "Don't touch me."

Chapter Two

Tracy's eyes flew to David at Kent's unexpected outburst, but David was watching Kent, a frown deepening his gaze.

"Sorry, Kent," David said quietly, stepping back. "I shouldn't have done that."

Kent's stiff shoulders slumped down and he turned away. "Can I come after school to see my kitty?" he mumbled.

"Of course you can." Tracy balled her hands into fists, stifling the urge to stroke his hair away from his eyes, soothe the emotions that flitted across his face.

She looked up to see David watching her, his deep-set eyes enigmatic, his expression serious. Again their eyes held and once more a whisper of caring wafted across the distance.

She gave him a careful smile.

"I'll get you those gloves," she said, turning away. "Then I'll go."

* * *

By the time they were inside Kent's apartment building, he was relaxed, chatting about his kitten as if the outburst with David hadn't happened.

"This is where I live," Kent said stopping in front of a door with no number. The walls beside the door were grimy and the doormat was worn. "I have to find something secret, so you have to look away."

Tracy obediently turned her back, looking down at the stained carpet. She heard the snick of the key in the lock, waited for Kent to "hide" his key again and then turned around.

"You have to wait outside," Kent said putting his hand on the doorknob.

Tracy understood his innate caution. In spite of the surprising affection she felt for this young boy, to him she was still an adult stranger. "You might want to take a minute to brush your hair."

"Why?" Kent asked, glancing back.

Then he suddenly fell forward as the door was pulled out of his hand.

"What is going on here?" A woman stood in the doorway, her hair a brown nest, her eyes raccoon-ringed with smudged black mascara. Distinct lines were pressed into the sharp features of her cheek and temple. A sloppy, oversize T-shirt hung halfway to her knees. "Kent, what are you doing out of the apartment?" Her voice was still raspy with sleep.

"I just wanted to go outside, Mom," he explained, his voice growing smaller, his head dropping.

Kent's mother grabbed him by the shoulder and

yanked him past her into the still-darkened apartment. "You go get ready for school." She turned back to Tracy. But Kent stopped just beyond her, watching them both.

His mother crossed her arms over the faded T-shirt. "What were you doing with my boy?" She snapped the words out.

"I work at the clinic down the road," Tracy said. She held the woman's gaze, yet was aware of the curtains pulled across the windows, the clothes scattered over the floor of the dimly lit apartment. A weary, depressive atmosphere oozed out of the room, making Tracy shiver with memories. "Kent came and visited us this morning," she said, carefully guarding Kent's secret.

"He shoulda told me. I was worried sick."

Tracy doubted she had lost any sleep over her son. She looked as though she had just rolled out of bed.

"I brought him home so he could get ready for school." Tracy didn't mention the time.

"I always take him." The words were thrown out like a challenge.

"Of course," Tracy murmured. Kent stood with his head bowed, his hands clasped in front of him, a premonition of fear catching her.

She wanted to grab him and run. Take him to her home. Feed him a solid meal, take care of him. Stave off whatever was going to happen to him when the door closed.

All she could do was smile at him, hope and pray that he would sense her concern. That she would have a chance to create some trust in her. "You take care, Kent. Have a good day in school."

Kent glanced quickly at his mother, who scowled back at Tracy. But just before the door closed, Kent gave her a hesitant smile.

Tracy thought about him all the way back to the clinic. *Please, Lord, watch over that helpless child. Let me maintain some kind of contact with him. Keep an eye on him.*

For now, praying was all she could do.

"You were quick." Crystal's sharp voice greeted Tracy as she entered the office. "Thought you were taking that kid to school?"

Tracy pulled a lab coat off a hanger and threaded her arms through it. "His mother said she would." She tried to ignore her own concerns, hoping Kent dared to come to the clinic again. "Did I miss any calls?"

Crystal leaned forward, her heavy arms crowding her ample bosom. "So you and David had some time together this morning." She leaned forward, her eyes gleaming. "Hope it was quality time?" She dragged the last two words out, heavy with innuendo.

Tracy ignored Crystal's blatant comments. She was having enough trouble trying to sort out her feelings for David, she didn't need Crystal stirring them up. "We were working, Crystal."

Crystal flipped her comments off with a casual wave of her hand. "That tousled blond hair, those deep-set eyes, that crooked mouth." She sighed. "I could think of better things than work."

Thankfully, Tracy heard the phone ring, cutting off any further conversation. Crystal answered it, then covered the handset, handing it to Tracy.

"Edgar Stinson," she whispered, pushing away from the desk. "I'll be in the supply room."

Tracy took the phone, her heartbeat kicking up a notch. Anticipation threaded with a low note of dread sang through her as she raised the phone to her ear.

"Tracy here."

"Stinson. You told me to call you at the vet clinic. So I'm calling."

Tracy lowered herself into the chair Crystal had vacated, her knees wobbling. She sent up another quick prayer, drew in a shaky breath.

For the past two years she'd been trying to make a deal with Edgar Stinson for an old abandoned yard site that took up one corner of the many quarter sections of land he owned. Available acreages within reasonable driving distance of Preston were scarce. It had taken many diplomatic phone calls, a few visits and constant gentle cajoling to get him even to consider subdividing.

Tracy put on her most pleasant voice. "Thanks for calling me back." She clutched the receiver of the phone, struggling to suppress her excitement.

"I thought about that acreage you wanted. You can have it."

The import of the words took time to register. As they did, Tracy exhaled slowly, the nebulous dreams she'd hardly dared entertain finally finding a solid resting ground. *Thank you, Lord,* she prayed, relief making her limbs rubbery. "That's great. I'm so glad to hear that." She bit back the flow of gratitude. Edgar Stinson had made it quite clear he was treating this as a business transaction and didn't want any fawning.

"Only thing," he continued, "They want one thousand dollars. To subdivide it. You can pay that."

Tracy could hardly keep up with his staccato comments. But she caught one phrase very distinctly. "One thousand dollars?"

"You heard me. Write me a check."

A faint note of caution sounded deep in her mind. "If I do that, I was wondering if we could draw up an Agreement for Sale?" she asked quietly.

"You don't trust me?" Edgar Stinson's voice exploded through the phone.

Tracy clutched the handset with one sweaty hand, her other hand toying with the button on her lab coat as she chose her next words as carefully as if she were plucking wild Alberta roses from their thorny bushes.

"It's just business, Mr. Stinson. If I'm paying the subdividing costs you can appreciate that I'm going to need some assurance myself." *Please, Lord, let him agree to that. At least that.*

"No legal yikyak. You want the acreage, you pay the costs. Simple as that." Each word he spoke was more unyielding than the last.

Tracy wavered, knowing her moment of silence could be interpreted wrongly by this volatile man.

But the lure of her own place, a piece of land she might build a house on, make the home she had yearned for all her life, pulled her past her own objections and stilled the practical voice that balked at putting out money for nothing.

"Okay. I'll give you a check."

"I'll meet you at the inn sometime in the next couple of days to get it. While we're talking, you tell that new vet David to give me a call. He came yesterday. Killed my cow." And with an ominous click, he rang off.

Tracy gently laid the phone in the cradle, as if offsetting Edgar Stinson's rudeness. She scribbled a note for David. Then, on another piece of paper, she wrote the amount Mr. Stinson had requested. One thousand dollars.

Was she crazy to willingly sacrifice such a large amount of money without any guarantee?

"He'll sell it to me. I know he will," Tracy muttered aloud as if putting sound to the words spinning through her head made them more real. She shoved her fingers through her hair and clutched her skull.

Before Tracy could think too much more about it, the buzzer announced another customer just as the phone started ringing again.

For the next eight hours Tracy didn't have time to sit down, much less think about the money Mr. Stinson wanted. A crippled horse kept her and David busy until coffee time, then a spay, a neuter and a trip with Dr. Harvey out to a farm to do some preg testing. Then back to the clinic to try to catch up on bookkeeping. In a larger clinic the vets would hire a bookkeeper but in a clinic this size the vet techs did double duty. Because Crystal was the senior tech, those duties usually fell to Tracy. Between all that, she had been checking on Kent's kitten, making sure it was still alive.

By the time she put up the closed sign at the end of the day, Mr. Stinson's demand was only a hazy number hovering in the back of her mind.

She closed the door and turned around to see David lounging by the reception desk, still wearing his coveralls.

"That kitten's looking pretty good. I just want to tell you to keep an eye on that leg. I'm scared he's going to bust those stitches if we can't keep him immobilized."

"Sure." She gave him a quick smile as she slipped past him to get to the desk. His presence dominated the room, and, as she glanced up at him again, she was disconcerted to see those hooded eyes looking at her.

"So, you off to see Danielle again?" he asked.

"Our usual Monday-night date." She dropped the key in the desk and slid it shut. "We've been doing it for years."

"Friends are good."

She looked up at the faintly wistful tone in his voice. "Are you getting to know a few people?"

"Some. It takes time in a small town. I should learn to play golf. Apparently that helps."

"You might want to start small."

He winked at her. "Getting there. I'm working on my mini golf game but the dreaded windmill still eludes me."

"Many a good man has been tripped up on that one," she said, his gentle teasing drawing an answering smile.

He held her gaze, a sense of expectation hovering between them, then he disappeared into his office.

Voices old and new reminded her: Be careful. Guard your heart. No one else is going to take care of you.

But, as she slipped on her sweater and caught up her purse, she felt as though she were warning herself more out of habit than conviction,

By the time she got to the Preston Inn, Danielle was

already waiting, looking relaxed for a change. Usually she came bustling in from some emergency or crisis that had demanded her immediate attention. Today she sat in the booth, staring out the window, twisting a strand of her long, blond hair around her finger. She'd already slipped out of her business-suit jacket, her peach-colored blouse softening the austere cut of her skirt.

"Sorry I'm late." Tracy slipped into their usual booth, smiling apologetically. Danielle glanced at her friend and smiled.

"Wasn't waiting long."

"You must have had a very slack day to be able to quit so soon."

Danielle's cheerful expression faded. "Wish that were true. I had to do an apprehension of a young girl early this afternoon. Her father threatened me. She tried to get out of the car while I was driving. Cried and screamed all the way to the foster home. By the time I got her settled in, back to the office and done with the paperwork, I decided to cash in some of my unpaid overtime." Her slender fingers traced the embossed letters on the menu in front of her, her blue eyes softening.

Tracy recognized her friend's distress. Danielle put all of herself into her job as a social worker. Which was fortunate for the kids in her care, but not always so fortunate for Danielle.

"Hey, Dani." Tracy leaned across the table and touched her friend's arm. "What you're doing is important, okay? You did the background work on this family. She's probably more scared than anything. You're helping her. Giving her a chance to see what a good family can be like."

Danielle held her friend's gaze, the tightness around her mouth fading away. "And you should know, Tracy."

As Tracy shrugged off her comment and the memories that edged it, a picture of Kent slipped through her mind. She wondered where he was right now. What he was doing. She had hoped he would stop by the clinic after school, but he hadn't shown.

Maybe tomorrow morning.

The waitress came by, took their order and left again.

"So how was dear Anthony?" Tracy asked, as she settled into the comfortable predictability of Monday evening with her friend. "Your brothers said you went to visit him this weekend. They didn't sound impressed."

"The only thing that impresses them lately is a hemi," Danielle said with an unladylike snort of disgust.

"Hemi being?"

"Another kind of diesel motor." She dismissed the subject with a wave of her well-manicured hand. "Ask David. I would guess he's enough of a guy to know. Besides, it would give you and your broodingly handsome boss something else to talk about besides spays and neuters."

Tracy's neck grew warm at the implications inherent in Danielle's comment, and she tried to laugh her reaction off. "I don't know if I have time for something as deeply emotional as talking about truck motors." In spite of her flippant words, Tracy's renegade mind conjured up the image of David's large fingers gently touching the helpless kitten. The dimple that hovered around the edge of his smile. The casual wink he'd given her just before he left.

"Not all guys are like Art, Tracy. You know that."

"I know. But for now, he's just my boss, so leave it, please?"

To her surprise, Danielle's grin softened to an understanding smile. "But if he asks you out, just make sure you give him a chance, okay? You deserve some happiness."

"Well for now, my happiness is going to be tied up in my land. Edgar Stinson called."

Danielle's mouth fell open. "Really. And? Is he going to sell?" Danielle rotated her hand, encouraging more information.

"He is. But he wants a thousand bucks to pay subdividing costs."

"A thousand dollars? Surely that's not your responsibility?"

"Nope. But it could be a deal breaker for him."

"Are you sure you want to negotiate anything with him? He's so uncompromising."

Tracy lifted her hands in a gesture of defeat. "If I want that acreage, I don't have much choice. And I want that acreage."

"And the twelve chickens, the milk cow and the clothesline you told our grade-five teacher were your big dream in life," Danielle said with a soft smile, pulling out a memory.

"Don't forget the malamute."

"That was a more recent acquisition. Grade seven?"

"Six. Seven was the horse."

They chatted about Tracy's dream. Tracy pulled a pen and paper out of her purse and they spent the next few minutes laying out plans for pens, possibly a house to replace the one that burned down years ago on the yard site. They drew out where she could plant trees, decided on perennials.

Tracy was smiling when she looked up, and then she wasn't smiling anymore.

"What's the matter?" Danielle asked, following Tracy's glowering expression. Then sat back with a sigh. "Oh, I see."

Misty Bredo settled into a booth across the room, languidly toying with her hair, her bored expression saying more than words ever could.

"How long has she been back in town?" Tracy asked, tapping her pencil on the table.

"According to my brothers, only a couple of weeks."

"They would know." Tracy rapped the table once more, then turned back to her friend. "It's been three years since I caught her and Art together, yet seeing her can still make my blood boil."

"It wasn't a pretty moment."

"And my mother's little episode didn't help things either." Tracy shivered. "In a way I don't blame Art for picking Misty over me. He sure wouldn't have wanted to be grafted on to my tiny little family tree."

Tracy clamped her lips together as the waitress set their drinks in front of them.

"Well, at least he and Misty didn't last that long."

"A couple of weeks. The word *faithful* didn't seem to be in Art's dictionary."

"Well, if Art was half the man he should have been, he would have realized that he was dating you, not your mother. I've said it before, I'll say it again—you're better off without him."

"I know, I know. I'll just have to make sure to keep any future boyfriend far away from my mom, that's all." Tracy gave her friend a smile. "Not that that's been any huge problem lately.

But Danielle didn't return her smile.

"What's up, Dani? You're wearing your resolved expression."

Dani sighed lightly, giving her coffee another stir. "I was going to wait until after we ate."

A stillness drifted into Tracy's heart. "This sounds serious."

Danielle hunched her shoulders then looked directly at Tracy. "There was another reason I got here early. I wanted to be the first one to tell you. Velma called the office this afternoon."

Tracy felt the words dropping, one at a time, like cold stones into her midsection, distressing the fragile fabric of her life. "And what did my long-lost mother want?"

"To see you again." Danielle looked down at her cup. "She said she's changed her life. She left me her number."

Tracy willed her heart to stop its heavy beating. Willed her thoughts back to the constants in her life. Work. Church. Her friends. Memories of her mother still held claws that clung and hurt and she resented the need they created.

"I've heard that little ditty too often to believe it." Tracy pushed aside unwelcome thoughts and memories.

"When was the last time you saw her?" Danielle asked, cradling her cup between her hands.

"Two and a half years ago." Tracy swirled her milk around her glass, almost spilling it. "Six months after the Art fiasco. She stayed for about an hour, borrowed two hundred bucks and was gone again."

So hard not to sound bitter, to keep the anger out of her voice. Tracy thought she had conquered those insidious feelings of yearning and abandonment.

"I have an idea of what it's been like for you," Danielle said quietly. "But I also know that she still means something to you. It wouldn't hurt to give her a call. Just make it casual."

"There's never been 'casual' with Velma. Never ordinary. People have to be around more often for that to happen. And my mother wasn't." She clamped her lips together. If she kept talking she was going to sound as though she was feeling sorry for herself. A picture of Kent drifted into her mind.

"Subject switch," she said quickly, sitting up, gladly focusing on a concrete situation. "A little boy named Kent, about six or seven years old. Do you have any reports on him?"

"Are you going to call her?" Danielle asked quietly.

"No promises, Danielle. That subject is over." Tracy held up her hand forestalling the next comment she could already see forming on Danielle's lips. "Little boy. Named Kent."

"Okay, okay. What's his last name?"

"I don't know. He didn't tell me."

Danielle slowly shook her head, her lips pursed in thought. "Doesn't hit any notes with me. Why?"

"I've seen him walking by the clinic the past few

weeks on his way to school. This morning I caught him hanging around the clinic. He was poorly dressed, grubby and quite defensive for such a little scrap of a kid."

"You want me to start a file?"

Danielle reached for her purse and ever-present notebook, but Tracy shook her head. She wasn't sure she wanted to take it that far yet.

"Just keep him in mind. I'll be watching out for him, and I'll let you know if I find anything else out. I'm worried about him."

Chapter Three

"The cow was beyond my help." David moved the phone to his other ear and closed the door of Dr. Harvey's office to give him privacy. "I should've been there an hour sooner to do any good." He kept his voice neutral, his tone careful as he sat in the chair by the desk.

"I want that bill ripped up," Mr. Stinson growled. "I already talked to your worker, Tracy, about it yesterday. It's a crazy amount of money. I'm not paying for treatment on a dead cow."

The easiest solution would be to simply write off the expense, but a cursory check on previous bills to Edgar Stinson brought up a disturbing pattern. Constant complaints, bills reduced and at times nullified.

"I'm sorry the cow died, Edgar," he said firmly. "But I can only work with what I'm given. I did what you wanted when you called me out. I have to charge you for that."

Deafening silence greeted this declaration. Then a harsh click resounded in his year.

Score one for diplomacy, David thought hanging up the phone. He dragged his hands over his face and blew out his breath. He knew how precarious his place in this new community was. The meticulous building of a reputation happened by slowly gaining trust one case at a time. Coffee-shop complaints carried a lot of weight in a small town.

He pushed himself away from the desk. He'd done the right thing. He just had to hold his ground and hope that Crystal and Tracy would help him in this.

Voices caught his attention and with a faint lifting of his spirits he followed the sounds.

Kent and Tracy were in the kennel room. Tracy was crouched down in front of the cage that held Kent's kitten.

"Why can't he get up?" Kent asked, his hands tucked in the pockets of the same worn jeans he'd had on yesterday. His T-shirt looked a little better, though not much warmer against the chill of the day.

"See, we keep him lying down like that so his bones can heal," Tracy said. And, as David watched, her fingers feathered the boy's hair away from his forehead in a motherly gesture. To his surprise, the little boy allowed it.

As if sensing his presence, Tracy glanced back over her shoulder.

Her unexpected smile cancelled some of the negative energy Edgar Stinson had pressed into his day. At least with Tracy things were looking up.

"The kitten is looking pretty good this morning," Tracy said, pushing herself to her feet. "I was just telling Kent what we did."

Kent spun around and David was disappointed to see his wary look edge back. Kent looked down at the floor, moving closer to Tracy. "Tracy says you fixed my kitty real good and I'm s'posed to say thank-you," he mumbled.

"You're welcome. I know Tracy will take good care of it for you."

"I forgot to tell you," Tracy said, "but Mr. Stinson phoned yesterday. He was unhappy about his dead cow."

Unhappy didn't quite cover the fury that Edgar had spilled out on the phone. "I talked to him already. Tried to tell him that calcium alone wouldn't have saved that cow. Only going back in time would have."

"Not your specialty?"

"Didn't do too well in Time Travel 220," he said with a grin, responding to the teasing note in her voice. "Spent too much time in Overcharging the Customer 101."

Tracy's laugh lifted his heart from its steady beat.

Their eyes met and held and as the moment length ened he felt poised on the brink of deeper emotions. And behind that he recognized a wedge of guilt when he thought of Heather's family and what was coming up.

"I hafta go," Kent said, tugging on Tracy's lab coat.

She blinked, looked down and the moment was whisked away.

"I can take…"

"I'll walk…"

David and Tracy spoke at once, then both stopped.

"I'll walk him to school," Tracy said, slipping off her coat.

But Kent shook his head wildly. "No. You can't come

with me." He took a step away, then before either of them could say or do anything, he was out the door and running down the hall.

"Kent. Wait." David went after him, but the little boy ran even faster. When David stepped out of the clinic, he could see Kent's tiny figure running down the road toward the school.

The boy's panic was unnatural. Disturbing. As was his constant wariness around him. "Flighty little guy, isn't he?" he said to Tracy who had followed him out of the clinic. "Hope he's not too scared to come back."

"He'll be back. He's very attached to that kitten." Tracy hunched her shoulders against the chill breeze that swirled around the front of the clinic. "Though I'm not sure he can take it home. He can barely take care of himself."

"You might end up the proud owner of a purebred mongrel," David said, stepping back into the warmth of the clinic.

"I'll have to move if that's the case. No pets allowed in my apartment." Tracy gave him a wistful smile as they walked back to her desk.

Then why had she offered to pay for the kitten's care? Which reminded him of another thorny issue.

"I need to talk to you about Edgar Stinson's account," he said.

Tracy sent a defensive glance his way.

He couldn't think of a diplomatic way to say what he had to, so he plunged right in. "I noticed he gets quite a few discounts."

"You've been checking the bookkeeping?"

Definitely defensive.

"I'm a partner in this business, Tracy. The finances are just as important as the vet work," he said quietly, hoping his soothing voice would smooth things over.

"You could have asked me what you needed to know." Not hard to hear the resentment in her voice, but he couldn't let that stop him.

"I thought that was what I was doing."

"Mr. Stinson has quite a bit of influence in this town."

"In other words, don't buck him?" David didn't like what he was hearing. "That makes Preston sound like a grade-B Western with Edgar Stinson the local land baron."

"Life imitates art," Tracy said dryly. "I'd be just a bit careful around him."

"Warning taken. But I'd prefer it if you and Crystal discuss any future discounts with me as well as Dr. Harvey."

"Okay." She spun around and flipped open the checkbook, dismissing him with her actions.

So much for impressing Miss Harris today, David thought with a light sigh. Why did he bother?

Because there's something intriguing about her. Because she's got a softness that comes through unexpectedly at times.

Because sometimes you just can't explain attraction even when the timing is all wrong.

As David stepped into the foyer of the church the dull noise of Sunday conversation washed over him. Clusters of people familiar with each other laughed and exchanged stories as they pulled mail from the bank of mailboxes along one wall. Two young boys, hair slicked Sunday-smooth, shrieked past him with an older girl in heated pursuit.

Like a wave, frowns of older people followed the boys' progress then disappeared as people were drawn back into conversation with their neighbors.

A familiar blond head caught his eye and with a flash of guilt, he recognized her. What was Emily doing here? She hadn't told him she was coming. He had secretly hoped to connect with Tracy. That wasn't going to happen if Emily was here.

"Welcome to our service, David."

A hand caught his arm lightly then let go as he turned to face a young woman in a flowing blue dress. The fluorescent overhead lights gilded her copper hair, brushed her smooth, pale complexion.

But he couldn't place her.

She sensed his confusion. "My name is Joanne. I brought my bird in to you last week."

His mind scrambled through the cases from the previous week. Avian parasite, he thought with a flush of relief. "So how is your parakeet?"

"Fine now. Thanks." Her soft green eyes flicked to his, then away. "How are you enjoying living in Preston?"

Before he answered he gave the foyer another sweep, but he hadn't seen Tracy yet. "I like it," he said, turning his attention back to Joanne. "It's a good place. Good people." Blank words spilling out of a preoccupied mind.

"There you are." A familiar voice was both his rescue and his doom. He turned to see Emily who had slipped her arm through his and pulled him down for a quick kiss. "I'm so glad to see you. I thought we might have missed you."

"No. I come every week." He tried not to fidget. Tried not to let his gaze wander back to the door as it opened and a few more people came in.

Emily was looking at Joanne with undisguised interest. "Hello, Joanne. How's your work going?"

"Just fine. It's spring, so it's crazy busy." Joanne's eyes flicked from David to Emily, her finely plucked eyebrows lifted in a faint question as she tried to make the connection between them.

"Joanne is our accountant." Emily explained to David, tugging lightly on his arm, drawing him away. "Sorry to steal David from you, but I'd like him to meet some friends of ours."

"I understand you practiced in Grande Prairie before?" Joanne said to David, undeterred by Emily's discourtesy.

David should not have been surprised at her knowledge. Word didn't get around this small town, it flew. "I grew up there."

"Really? I lived there when I was young." Joanne turned to Emily, giving her a careful smile. "Didn't you come from there as well?"

"My parents live there," Emily said quickly, her pressure on his arm increasing slightly.

"I didn't know that. What are their names?"

"Stanley and Linda Verheeg."

Joanne frowned. "Verheeg? That name is so familiar." She tapped her fingers against her jaw, then spread her hand out in an I-know gesture. "Didn't they have a daughter who died of cancer about a year ago…?" Joanne stopped, her eyes wide as she pressed her fingers to her mouth. "I'm sorry, Emily. Heather Verheeg would have been your sister."

Emily's fingers dug into his arm, expressing a sorrow that was almost as strong as the guilt David felt at his inability to match it.

"She was. Now if you'll excuse us." This time Emily made no pretense at politeness, and this time when she pulled on his arm, David followed her.

"I'm sorry, David," Emily's voice wavered. "Are you okay?"

He was. But he knew that wasn't what Emily wanted to hear. "It's always hard to think about Heather," he said quietly.

"You two were so happy together," Emily said, discreetly wiping a tear from her eye. "I can't believe it's been a whole year." She sniffed and pulled David closer, as if seeking comfort from him.

"Me neither." David returned Emily's hug, then gently drew away. Once again he looked around and once again found no sign of Tracy. This time it was a good thing. He'd had no idea Emily was going to be here.

A definite complication.

"Jack. Look who I found," Emily said as they approached a tall man holding the hands of two children.

The man's smile was warm. Friendly. David knew that Emily's husband Jack would be a little easier to deal with than the still-sniffing Emily.

"Are you going to sit with us, Uncle David?" Rachel, Emily's daughter slipped around her father and punched David lightly on the arm.

Thankful for the distraction, David glanced down at Emily's daughter and tweaked her nose.

"Are you sure you want to sit with an old man like me?"

Rachel rolled her eyes with all the expertise of a young girl on the cusp of her teens and gave him another punch. "Whatever."

"What's with that?" David complained with mock seriousness, thankful for a return to ordinary. "A new way to tell me you love me?" He gave her a quick one-armed hug.

"Uncle David, you're totally messing up my hair."

"You want to see messing?" David let his hand hover over her hair, grinning down at Rachel's horrified face.

"Excuse me, please."

The quiet voice drew him around. And there stood Tracy Harris, trying to edge past him.

"Hello, Tracy."

Her head jerked up, a light frown furrowed her smooth brow. Then as she recognized him, a faint smile played along her lips.

"Hello yourself," she said, her brown eyes holding his. Her hand came up to fiddle with the top button of her shirt. Its vibrant peach color enhanced her tanned features, emphasized her dark hair. She looked beautiful.

"So you decided to come this morning?" he asked.

Very slick, David. Very suave. Keep smiling and she won't think you're a complete idiot. Just a partial one.

"I usually do." Her smile held a teasing note now.

"I didn't see you last Sunday. I sat in the back. The week before that I visited my father back in Grande Prairie." David's brain scrambled, trying to come up with something wittier than a listing of his travel agenda.

"Then welcome to our fellowship," Tracy said, running her hands up and down the leather strap of her purse. She smiled at Rachel and was about to turn away.

Before he could stop himself, he detained her, placing his hand on her shoulder. "I'm sorry, Tracy. I'm losing my manners," he said as she turned back, her eyebrows lifted as if questioning him.

"This is my niece Rachel. She lives in Kolvik with my..." he stumbled over his relationship to Heather's sister "...with Emily and her husband Jack, her parents." David glanced down at Rachel, hoping she would cooperate. "Rachel, this is Tracy Harris. She works with me at the clinic."

"Hello, Rachel." Tracy held out her hand and Rachel took it reluctantly, glancing at David as if asking him why he was making her talk to this older lady.

"What do you do for my uncle David?" Rachel asked, putting a polite smile on her face as she made the requisite small talk.

What a doll. David gave Rachel's shoulder an encouraging squeeze.

"Some interesting things. And some ordinary things." Tracy's gaze glanced over at David, back to Rachel as if trying to figure out the uncle part. "The other day we sewed up a kitten's leg."

Tracy's gaze met his, her features softened by her smile and once again he found himself drawn to her.

"Hey, David." Emily slipping her arm through his. "We should sit down."

David glanced back at her, stifling his momentary annoyance. "Be with you in a minute."

But when he turned back to Tracy, she was walking away from him.

Tracy tapped her fingers restlessly against her crossed arms, her eyes searching the sanctuary for Danielle.

"Looking for a spot, Tracy?" The usher, a trim, dapper man of about seventy was beside her, handing her a printed order of worship and a bulletin of church news and events.

"Have you seen Danielle Hemstead, Mr. Henderson?"

The older man shook his head, the overhead lights glinting off his shiny scalp. "I'm afraid not. There are some empty spots on the other side of the sanctuary. She might be there."

Tracy stood up on tiptoe, trying one last time to find Danielle. Nothing. She turned back to the usher with a light sigh of resignation. "Just make sure you don't seat me too close to the front." She disliked parading down the aisle.

Mr. Henderson gave her a conspiratorial smile. "I've got just the place."

He led her, in his slow, hitching step, along the back of a bank of pews, down the aisle, then he stopped by an open seat at the end of a bench. Tracy faltered when she saw the other occupants of the pew.

David and his family. Or whatever they were.

She spied another empty seat, farther up, that she would have preferred to sit in. But it would have been rude to simply walk past Mr. Henderson.

So she slipped into the bench, flashing a quick glance sideways, but David was leaning over Rachel and hadn't seen her yet. She unfolded the bulletin, reading over the events of the week, notices of a bake sale, a thank-you from Christa and Jordan Payne for the lovely shower gifts. But the longer she looked down, the harder it became to ignore David.

Then out of the corner of her eye, she saw Rachel point at her. Saw David's head turn.

At that moment, the praise group started up. The congregation rose to its feet as people gradually joined in.

David had a deep voice. Pleasant. He sang along easily, his fingers tapping out the tune on the pew in front of him.

Once in awhile she sensed his eye on her, but she resolutely kept her gaze on the screen, as if seeing the words for the first time. Sitting beside him had not been a good idea. She was more aware of him than she liked.

At the end of the last song, the pastor bounded up the steps to the pulpit and welcomed everyone. "And I'd like you to extend the hand of welcome to the people around you this morning."

There was the usual momentary confusion of people turning around to face the backs of the persons behind them who were also turning around. Tracy shook the hands of the Marsden family in front of her, the O'Toole twins behind her, then finally dared to turn to David.

He was talking to a young couple in front of him, but his gaze skittered sideways, catching hers as if he had been waiting for her.

"Welcome, Tracy." His handclasp was as firm as she knew it would be.

"That should be my line," Tracy said with a light laugh. "Even though you've been here four months, according to Preston you're the visitor, I'm supposed to be welcoming you."

"That's right. This is your hometown."

David smiled at her and Tracy realized that David still held her hand. She was suddenly aware of the warmth of it, of how hers was swallowed up in his, his large fingers curling around hers.

Once again she felt as if his deep-set eyes had captured hers, pulled her into the very essence of him.

This was getting a little dangerous.

She pulled her hand out of his, but David seemed loathe to end the conversation.

"I checked on Kent's kitten this morning," he said. "He's looking good."

"Do you want me to check him later on today?"

"No. I'll run by tonight."

"That would be great."

"Did your mother used to attend this church with you?" He asked.

The mention of her mother was a splash of cold reality.

"When she was around we did." Tracy turned away from David, fumbling for the songbook as the pastor announced the first song. Resentment thrummed through her as she flipped through the pages. Velma again. A throb of what she had felt her whole childhood returned. A dull pain woven of many smaller sorrows.

Tracy had found respite from her past in the present. In God's faithful love. Allowing her mother in her life now meant opening herself to more disappointment and hurt.

Tracy had promised herself after all the ineffective tears she'd shed over her mother and Art that no one was ever going to make her cry again.

Tracy concentrated on the song, allowing it to still the other words in her heart. Words that condemned her as unworthy. As unimportant. The song pulled her close to God's side. She had perfect love unending beyond all knowledge and all thought available to her. Surely that should be enough.

The service flowed along, the familiar liturgy and responses creating a rhythm that gave her sanctuary from her thoughts, a sanctuary she had discovered the first time she had been invited to church by Danielle.

The scripture reading was from Colossians 3. Tracy opened her Bible, followed along.

"'Therefore, as God's chosen people, holy and dearly beloved,'" the pastor read "'clothe yourselves with compassion, kindness, humility, gentleness and patience. Bear with each other and forgive whatever grievances you may have against one another. Forgive as the Lord forgave you…'"

Tracy read the words, stopped and read them again. Words so familiar had suddenly become heavy with expectations.

She thought of Kent and the key he carried around his neck. The same place she had carried hers.

I can't do this yet, she thought, closing her eyes as she clutched the spine of her Bible. *Dear Lord, I don't have the strength to deal with my mother. I'm getting somewhere with my own life. I can't let her in.*

She looked up, past the people in the pews in front of her, beyond the pastor to the stained-glass window above him. Diffused sunlight brought the window to sparkling life, spreading its jewel colors over the congregation like a benediction. Tracy felt as if she was reaching out to God, trying to understand what He wanted from her. She drew in a slow breath and turned away from the window. Unconsciously her glance slid sideways.

David was watching her, a bemused expression on his face. She looked down at her Bible, pressing it against her. David was another complication she was unsure about right now. Being attracted to David was the fast track to heartbreak. She had nothing to give him.

Only God is faithful. Only God.

Chapter Four

"May as well bring this thing straight to the auto wrecker." The Monday-morning death sentence on her car was delivered without emotion by Chip Hemstead, a stocky young man with two earrings in each ear and a tattoo of a snake slithering down his thick body-builder's neck.

Danielle's youngest brother.

"You don't think it's worth fixing?"

"You're gonna need a new head. My guess the tranny is gone and the rad's all gummed up with stop-leak. It's toast." Chip had done all of Tracy's mechanic work so he had first-hand experience with her car. And her do-it-yourself mechanic work. "Time to move on. Treat yourself to a new ride. I know how you squirrel away money. You can afford it."

"Not really," she said as panic edged around her mind. "I'm going to need every penny I can scrounge together once I buy that land. I figured on my poor car lasting me a little longer than this."

"Dani said you had some kind of deal in the works. How's it comin'?"

"It's coming." After she coughed up one thousand dollars to Edgar Stinson. She had arranged to meet him tomorrow to discuss it further, though she still wasn't sure what she was going to tell him.

"Good stuff. You were always good with the dollars." Chip pulled into the parking lot and Tracy was disappointed to see it was empty. "Have a good 'un, Trace," he said as she got out.

As he roared away, Tracy unlocked the clinic door. She liked these quiet moments in the morning before everyone came, though in the past few weeks David had been showing up earlier, arriving right on her heels.

In a few minutes she had the coffeepot on and clean mugs set out, settling herself in her early-morning routine.

She pulled open the fridge to pull out a packet of doughnuts she had brought in yesterday.

It was gone.

Puzzled she checked the cupboards, but all she found was the usual sugar and coffee containers. And an empty cookie bag that had been full on Saturday. This was getting strange.

When she went to check the animals the kennel door was open. Frowning Tracy stepped inside. A faint whine issued from one of the cages, a rustling from another. Then a scrambling sound and in the half light, Tracy saw a shadow slide along the far wall.

"Who's there?" she called sharply, her heart kicking

into high gear. "Come out so I can see you." She flicked on the light, but stayed in the doorway, poised to run if she had to.

"It's just me." A tiny figure stepped slowly out into the light, his head bent.

"Kent. What are you doing here?" Tracy forced herself not to rush to his side. To catch him close. "How did you get in?"

He jabbed at a hole in his T-shirt with one finger, viciously twisting it around. "I sneaked in."

Undeterred by the belligerence in his voice, Tracy stopped in front of him, dropping to one knee. "How did you do that?" What was he doing here? Why wasn't he home? Did his mother know? Care?

But she kept her voice quiet as she laid a gentle hand on his shoulder.

"Yesterday. When that David man came. I put a stick in the door." He looked up at her now, his dark eyes wide, pleading, a complete contrast to the defensive tone she'd heard just moments ago. "I wanted to see my kitty…and…I was tired and…" He stopped.

"And what, sweetie?"

When he didn't reply an uncomfortable thought pushed itself forward. "Did you sleep here last night, Kent?"

He nodded. "I found some blankets." He looked up, the challenge back in his voice. "I stole some doughnuts too."

Tracy ignored his bluster, recognizing the fear it hid. "That's okay, sweetie. Don't worry." Tracy tried to smile her assurance past a face tight with anger as she imagined how frightened he must have been to end up here.

A noise behind them made his head jerk up, the fear

flashing across his face quickly replaced by an almost feral look. Tracy spun around.

David stood framed in the doorway. "Hey, there," he said, coming closer. Tracy looked back at Kent, wondering if he was going to run again. "Was that your car behind the tow truck that just left?"

"Yes. It broke down." Tracy kept her gaze on Kent, who was edging away from David.

"You're here early," David said to Kent. "Have you seen your kitten yet?"

Kent's eyes skittered over David then back to Tracy as if to see what she was going to say. He only nodded.

"That's good." David glanced at Tracy, lifting one eyebrow in amusement. "So what are you doing here this time of the morning?"

Tracy held his gaze a split second longer than she had to. She could ask him the same question, but didn't dare. "Just came to check on Kent's kitten," she said gently. She turned back to Kent, touching him lightly on the shoulder. "You probably came so early you forgot to eat breakfast." She winked at him, as if signaling their conspiracy.

He nodded, his cautious gaze on David.

"How about I take you to the restaurant and buy you pancakes?" Tracy said. He needed more in him than just doughnuts.

Kent shrugged lightly, but looked up at her. "I hafta ask my mom."

Tracy doubted she was around, but went along with a charade. "Why don't we give her a call?"

"Can I come too?" David asked. "You'll need a ride."

The idea held a certain appeal, but she looked down at Kent who was still twisting his T-shirt around his finger. "It depends on Kent."

Kent looked up at Tracy as if for confirmation.

"He's a nice man," Tracy said. "He won't hurt you."

Kent licked his lips, then gave an imperceptible nod of affirmation.

"I guess you just got the seal of approval, David," Tracy said.

His deep-set eyes held hers, a smile curving his shapely mouth. "You'll need a ride to get there."

"But we hafta ask my mom," Kent repeated, his little voice firm.

"Sure, sport," David said, still crouched down. "I think that's a good idea."

But it turned out Kent's diligence wasn't necessary.

"There's no answer," Tracy said, disconnecting after the twelfth ring. Kent chewed his lip, still hesitating. "I'm sure it will be okay," Tracy assured him.

He sighed lightly and Tracy could hear the faint rumbling of his stomach.

"So let's go," she said brightly, smiling at Kent and taking his hand. To her surprise, he allowed it.

His slightly sticky fingers clasped around hers surprised a quiver of tenderness in her. She clutched his hand, and, as she smiled down at him, she allowed the emotion to take root. To grow. Kent was much safer than David, she thought with a wry smile. He probably wouldn't break her heart.

But as David walked up beside her, she couldn't help but wonder if David might not either.

* * *

"Your eggs won't run away," Tracy teased, holding Kent's hand down before he shoved another forkful of food into his mouth.

Kent's gaze darted to David, his expression wary, as if waiting to see what David would say. David gave him a cautious smile of approval, concerned over the boy's hypervigilance around him.

"You're going to get a bellyache if you don't eat more slowly," David said quietly, hoping he didn't sound too bossy.

Kent looked at Tracy as if for confirmation. "Is he right? Will I get sick if I eat too fast?"

"It could happen."

Satisfied that David might be right, Kent returned to his food, pacing himself a little better.

"Can I see my kitty after school today?" Kent mumbled around a mouthful of pancake.

"Of course you can," Tracy said. "If that's okay with your mom."

"I can keep it a secret," Kent said quietly as he finished the last of his breakfast. "My mommy makes me keep secrets all the time."

David felt a flash of concern at the same time that he caught Tracy's startled glance.

"You don't have to keep this a secret, Kent," Tracy said. "I don't want your mom to be angry with us."

"And you should go wash your hands, Kent. You need to get to school," David said, glancing at his watch.

"We'll wait for you," Tracy said pulling his chair back.

Kent jumped down and ran off to the bathroom.

The waitress brought a wrapped sandwich Tracy had requested for Kent and the bill. David neatly intercepted it before Tracy could touch it. "You forgot it was my treat," he said pulling his wallet out.

Tracy gave him a quick smile, then glanced over her shoulder as if making sure Kent was out of range. "I don't know about you," she said folding her napkin, "but between finding him in the clinic this morning and that comment about secrets, I'm concerned."

"What can we do?"

Tracy folded her napkin again and creased it sharply. "I could call Danielle. She's a social worker. She could help."

David blew out his breath. "It might be a bit soon for that."

Tracy pressed her fingers down on the napkin, her nails almost white. "He was sleeping in the kennel room, David. He was all alone and hungry and scared." She looked up at David and he caught a glimpse of deep pain. "I don't think it's too soon at all."

Her unexpected vulnerability called to him, and he reached across the table, placing his hand on her arm, noting how soft her skin felt. How warm. She looked startled, but to his surprise, she didn't pull away. She held his gaze and as he held her arm a little tighter, a faint smile teased one corner of her mouth.

"I'm here again," Kent announced.

And to his disappointment, Tracy pulled away again. In some ways she could be so tough, but at these odd moments he sensed a vulnerability that echoed Kent's. It puzzled and intrigued him.

The drive back to the clinic was quiet. David had the stereo playing softly, the music creating a gentle ambience. Kent sat pushed up close to Tracy, keeping as much distance as possible between himself and David. When they got to the clinic Kent was about to jump out with Tracy but she stopped him, holding on to the open door. "Dr. Braun will drive you to school, Kent."

Kent wrapped his arms around his middle and rocked in his seat. "I don't wanna ride with Dr. David."

Tracy's expression softened as she touched him lightly on the nose and buckled him in. "It's okay, Kent. I told you, Dr. David is a good man."

Kent glanced over his shoulder and David gave him a careful smile, wondering how one went about looking nonthreatening and safe.

"We'll see you after school, little man," she said, then closed the door and stood by the front of the clinic, waving as they left. Just like a mother would.

"You have to remember, your puppy needs to have one of these pills every day." It was the next afternoon. Tracy held up the bottle for the little girl across the counter from her.

Kathleen wrinkled her very freckled nose in puzzlement. "How do I give it to him?"

"You'll have to put it in some food to trick him. Your mom can help you." Tracy dropped the vial of medication into a paper bag. As she handed it to the little girl she glanced at her mother, standing behind Kathleen. "It's not hard," Tracy said, her reassuring smile masking the nervous thump of her heart as she caught sight of the minute hand sweeping across the face of the large clock on the wall behind them.

Ninety-seven more minutes and she was meeting Edgar Stinson.

Seeing Kent's apartment, a vivid reminder of her own childhood, had made her even more determined to close this deal.

"Thanks for all your help, Tracy." Anna stroked her hand over Kathleen's hair. "We'll see if we can get Horace back to normal again."

Tracy watched Anna's pale fingers absently toying with the little girl's hair, lifting it, then smoothing it down. When Kathleen jerked her head lightly away Tracy wanted to catch the little girl by the shoulder. Tell her what a precious gift her mother had just given her and, based on the indulgent smile on Anna's face, gave Kathleen every day.

"Now you take as good a care of that puppy as your mom does of you and he'll be just fine," Tracy said instead.

Anna smiled at Tracy. "Thanks again." They walked to the door, but it burst open before they could reach it. Anna stepped out of the way of a very angry young woman wearing skin-tight, low-cut jeans and a belly-skimming beaded T-shirt. Tracy recognized her as soon as the door banged shut behind her.

"What do you think you're doin' with my kid?" Kent's mother strode up to Tracy's desk, her face a mask of fury. She wore her hair up today, emphasizing her sharp cheekbones, her garishly made-up eyes arched by a double pierced eyebrow. "Why you packin' him around? Feedin' him. Takin' him to school?"

Anna glanced worriedly over her shoulder and quickly ushered a very curious Kathleen out of the clinic as Tracy turned back to the furious woman.

She forced herself to stay calm. Be rational. Push down her own building anger at this woman's neglect. "Can you explain what the problem is?"

"I heard from a friend at the restaurant that you and some guy were givin' him breakfast." Kent's mother slapped her hand on the counter as if emphasizing her point, her hoop earrings swinging with each word she spat out. "You leave him alone or I'll call the cops on you."

If anyone had a right to call the police she and David did. But Tracy held the women's narrowed gaze and tried to let her seething anger roll past her. "I'm afraid I still don't know what the problem is. Mrs...." Tracy let the sentence hang, hoping this irate woman would introduce herself.

"It's Juanita and Kent is my kid and he ain't comin' here no more."

Tracy felt a pinch of unease. If Kent couldn't come to the clinic it was going to be harder to keep tabs on him. They needed more information. And Kent needed to know that he had a sanctuary here. Where would he go the next time his mother wasn't home? Because Tracy knew there would be a next time.

"He's been coming here because he brought a kitten here for us to look at. Could he at least come and see it?" Tracy forced herself to be reasonable. Tried to make it look as if the kitten was all that was at stake.

"He doesn't have a kitten." Juanita shook a warning finger in Tracy's face. "Stay away from him, you hear?

Just because you don't have kids of your own doesn't mean you can have mine."

"I think you had better be careful what you're saying," Tracy said quietly. How dare this woman come in here, throwing around accusations?

"You're wrong, lady. You're the one that has to be careful."

The sharp ring of the phone broke into the conversation.

Juanita slipped her hands into the back pocket of her blue jeans as she backed away from the counter. "You listen now. Stay away from my boy."

She spun around and was gone as quickly as she had come.

Tracy took a long slow breath, willing her own building anger to subside. She had to calm herself or the person on the other end of the phone was going to think they'd reached the wrong number.

The phone call was quickly dealt with. Another job for Crystal and Dr. Harvey to do while they were on the road.

The buzzer sounded and Tracy looked up to see a heavyset man come into the clinic, leading a dog whose nose resembled a jumbled pincushion.

"Let me guess," Tracy said, pushing away from the desk, glad for something concrete to do. "I'm looking at the loser in a fight with a porcupine."

The owner nodded, his own expression almost as lugubrious as the dog's. "I got up this morning and Radar here was sitting on the step, rubbin' his nose with his paw."

The dog raised its head to his owner's voice, his expression as distressed as a dog's could be.

The gentle interaction between dog and owner soothed Tracy's jangled nerves. It never failed to both amuse and surprise her how mushy some of the biggest, toughest men could be when it came to their animals.

"That porcupine really did a number on him, Mr. Allison." She gave him a reassuring smile. "I'll get Dr. Braun to look at him right away."

"Dr. Harvey is gone?"

"Dr. Braun is an excellent vet. Radar will be in good hands."

Dan Allison looked surprised at the defensive tone of her voice.

"Okay. It's just that Dr. Harvey always took care of Radar before."

"Dr. Harvey is out right now. Dr. Braun is very good." She stroked Radar's head then turned, almost bumping into David.

Suddenly self-conscious at her vehement defense of him, she took a quick step back, slipping her hands in the pockets of the loose smock she wore over her clothes. She jerked her head in Mr. Allison's direction, trying not to blush. "Could you have a look at this dog? Porcupine quills."

David's eyes glanced over her then back at the dog. "I see that. Have Mr. Allison bring him into one of the rooms. I'll be there."

Their eyes met. David smiled. And Tracy felt again that breath of hesitation that made her wonder, What if?

She looked away from David's appealing face. She had her own plans and her own dreams. Her What if? was in her own hands and it she was better off to keep it there.

"It will be awhile before we're done," Tracy said, turning to Mr. Allison, trying to sound businesslike. Trying not to pay attention to David's retreating footfalls. "Do you have other business in town?"

Mr. Allison nodded, about to pick up the dog when Tracy stopped him.

"That's okay. I'll get him." Tracy took the dog in her arms. "We'll take good care of him." Mr. Allison nodded, then left.

Tracy carried Radar to the back room and shouldered open the door.

David was already there, laying out a tray of supplies. He glanced up as Tracy laid the squirming dog on the table.

"I thought Mr. Allison was going to bring him in."

"Radar's not that big," Tracy said, holding the dog still, trying not to look up at David as he carefully pried open the dog's mouth.

"I'll need an injection of ketomin and valium made up," David murmured.

Tracy relaxed at the unemotional tone of his voice. Safer ground. "It doesn't look like any got too far down his throat," he added as she mixed up the anaesthetic. "Kelly forceps should do it."

She handed him the needle and watched as he injected Radar. The dog turned his head toward her as if wondering what was happening.

"You'll be okay," Tracy said, stroking the dog's head. "Just a little poke and when you wake up the awful quills will be gone."

David handed her the empty syringe and she gave

him the forceps as Radar slowly slumped to the table. Carefully David started working.

"So what was your take on Kent yesterday? I didn't get a chance to talk to you."

Tracy held the dog's head while her mind easily slipped back to Kent's mother's angry confrontation. "I still think we should contact social services," she said with more force than necessary.

Tracy pressed her lips together as flashes from her own past melded with the picture of Kent sleeping in the kennel room.

"I don't like that idea. Not until we can earn his trust and find out more about his situation."

But Tracy wasn't going to sit back and watch this young child's life go through the same humiliating routine hers had. "I'd like to file a report with Danielle. It doesn't mean anything is going to happen, but it is a start."

David shrugged, shifting the dog to get at some more quills. "I don't suppose that would hurt, though I don't want Kent to know. Or his mother."

"His mother stopped by this morning making all kinds of threats, yelling at me to stay away from her son. Quite the drama queen." Remnants of her anger with Kent's mother surfaced.

"When did that happen?"

"About twenty minutes ago. If she does what she threatened, we won't be seeing much more of Kent. That's why I don't want to wait too much longer."

"I doubt Danielle would have enough information to make a move on this case."

Tracy felt the anger slump out of her. "We can hardly

manufacture facts. Danielle needs hard and fast information in order to do something as drastic as remove Kent from his home."

"And if Kent isn't coming here anymore, it's going to be harder to find out what's going on," David murmured, tugging on a particularly stubborn quill.

Tracy steadied the dog's head as a familiar anger gripped her. If there was any way she could help Kent, she would.

"I guess we'll just have to find some way to keep an eye on him," Tracy said quietly. She couldn't help but sneak a quick look at the clock.

David caught her eye. "Something wrong?"

"I have an appointment with Edgar Stinson. I forgot to tell you."

"What about?"

"I'm buying an acreage from him. A long-held dream of mine." She delivered the information almost shyly, as if telling him gave him another connection to her.

"Good for you. When do you have to meet him?"

"In about an hour," she said, turning her attention back to the dog. "So I might be leaving a bit early."

"Are you working through a lawyer on this?"

Tracy pulled in a long slow breath, realizing how silly her actions looked laid out in front of David. "'No legal yikyak,' were his exact words." In spite of her nervousness, Tracy did a dead-on imitation of Edgar Stinson's nasal voice. David laughed.

"You sure you don't want to draw something up? Just in case?"

Tracy waggled her head as if weighing the information. It hit too closely to her own insecurities, yet she didn't want to antagonize Edgar on this. "We're not at the buying stage yet. All he wants is money to pay for the subdivision costs."

"Wouldn't hurt to cover yourself if your money is involved." David continued, as if playing on her wavering. "If he signs it, you've got leverage if he decides not to sell it to you. If he doesn't, you won't be any worse off than you are now."

As Tracy thought of the thousand dollars Edgar wanted, she realized David was right. Edgar had nothing to lose by signing something. She had too much to lose if he didn't.

"That's a good idea," she said, giving a grateful smile. "I'll put something nonthreatening together."

"I could help you if you want. I'm no legal expert, but I've gone through a few land deals." His forehead puckered in a light frown as he concentrated on extracting a pair of quills far down the dog's throat. "But if I can give you some nonlegal advice on Edgar Stinson, don't let him intimidate you."

"I wish he didn't, but he does." Tracy held up the tray for David to deposit the quills he had pulled out.

"Do you want me to come with you?"

His offer warmed her heart, but she shook her head. "I don't think Mr. Stinson likes you very much. Though I appreciate the offer, I don't think you would be an asset in the negotiation process."

David laughed as Tracy handed him the penlight. David shone it down the dog's throat, then picked up the forceps again.

"You're probably right." His eyes held hers as his expression became serious. "But I will give you one bit of advice. Edgar Stinson is a bully. Likes to brag that he plays hardball. Don't let him push you around. Don't let him threaten you. And don't be afraid to call his bluff."

Tracy held his steady gaze. "Thanks for the advice," she said quietly. "I'll try to put it in practice."

David turned his attention back to the dog. He carefully ran his hand inside Radar's mouth to make sure he hadn't missed any quills. Checked once more on the outside. Then he stripped off his gloves and dropped them in the garbage can.

"I'll take the dog back to the kennel room and then I'll see you out front." But before he lifted Radar off the table he touched her lightly, the merest whisper of his hand over her shoulder, but Tracy felt the warmth he kindled inside her growing.

Chapter Five

Half an hour later, Tracy stood in the entrance of the dining room of the Preston Inn, clutching the strap of her purse with sweaty hands. A quick glance around the half-empty tables showed that Edgar Stinson hadn't shown up yet.

"Waiting for someone, Tracy?" Jessica, one of the older waitresses, looked up from the coffee she was pouring for a customer. Her face held the world-weary air of a woman who had lived so long in one town that nothing surprised her anymore. She wore her graying hair short and her skirts even shorter.

"Edgar…" She stopped. Cleared her throat, suddenly nervous. "Edgar Stinson." She wished she felt more casual about the meeting. Wished that Edgar didn't have such a stranglehold on her dream.

It was a dream she'd cultivated her whole life, starting with small seeds hoarded from plans made when she was alone, cocooned in the silence of her apartment.

Plans that grew each time she visited Danielle's home on the farm in the country. Her fantasies of a place of her own became her feeble defense against the noises that intruded from the apartments beside, above and below. They were the one thing she could control.

Jessica straightened and looked around the dining room much as Tracy had. "I'm pretty sure he came in just a few minutes ago." She asked another waitress who slipped past the two of them. The girl angled her chin at an empty table with a chair pushed back from it. A worn plaid coat hung over the back, stained with grease at the cuffs and hem, the arms holding the bend of elbows, a ghostly memory of its wearer.

"He was sitting there. Must have gone out for cigarettes," the girl said, glancing at Tracy as if trying to decide what she would want from a man like Edgar Stinson.

"I can put you there until he comes," Jessica said, pointing her half-full coffeepot in the direction of the table, the dark-brown liquid sloshing around in the glass carafe.

"Thanks. That would be nice." Hardly nice. She didn't relish the idea of sitting in a haze of objectionable cigarette smoke trying to negotiate the most important deal of her life, but he had named the date and place.

"The usual chocolate milk, or can I convince you to take a walk on the wild side and get some tea?"

"The usual," Tracy said with a nervous smile.

As Jessica left, Tracy smoothed out the paper she had typed up in the clinic before she came here, disappointed to see her fingers trembling.

No legal yikyak.

The sample agreement she had drawn up with David's help hardly fell into that category. It was simple, straightforward and afforded her a flimsy protection should the unpredictable Edgar Stinson change his mind about the purchase.

The acrid smell of cigarette smoke intruded on her space just as a nasal voice pierced her thoughts.

"You're late." Edgar Stinson dropped into the chair across from her as he plucked the burning cigarette out of his mouth. He stubbed it in the ashtray and leaned his elbows on the table, grinning at her. His piercing blue eyes held a cunning that made Tracy shiver and wonder, once again, whether she was doing the right thing.

"So, you ready to play hardball?" he asked, his smile aiming at complete insincerity—with a sinister edge.

"I'm ready to talk about the land deal, yes," Tracy said, wishing her heart wasn't thundering so heavily in her chest. Wishing she didn't want this so badly. This man held too much power over her at the moment. She wished she had taken David up on his offer to come along.

"Did you bring the check?"

Tracy lifted her purse to her lap and fingered with the clasp, hesitating. "I did. But I before I give it to you…"

"You get it certified?"

"I didn't think that was necessary." With more confidence than she felt, Tracy pulled out the check she had carefully made out this morning, taking special care to write it clearly. Neatly. She unfolded it, kept one finger on it as she spun it around so Edgar Stinson could see the amount. "Here it is."

Edgar held her gaze a moment, as if testing her, then looked down at the check. Tracy could almost feel his eagerness to get his hands on it. And Tracy dared a little more, David's words giving her courage.

"I also drew up an agreement that I've already signed and would like you to as well. Just a small formality that covers my investment in the acreage."

Edgar's head snapped up as she pulled the papers out of her purse. The gleam was replaced by a piercing look. "I told you. No legal stuff."

"I just wrote this up myself. It's not a big deal. A copy for you and one for me." She held his gaze, willing herself not to back down. "We won't need to see a lawyer until we start dealing on the acreage."

He leaned forward, his nearness intimidating her. Just as David had said he would. She fought every instinct to lean back and away and forced herself to lean slightly forward into his space. Hold his steely gaze.

"Once it's subdivided. But till then, I ain't signing nothin', little lady. And if you want the land, you give me a certified check."

He's being unreasonable. Don't give in.

"I'm sorry. It's this or nothing." Where had that come from? Those brave bold words? But they were spoken and she couldn't take them back. Edgar held her gaze, testing her. A thin little smile tugged at his lips.

Edgar shoved his chair back, yanked his jacket off the back, almost upsetting it. "You push me too far, little lady." He paused a moment as if waiting for her to object.

The moment hung, tense, waiting. Don't give in. Call his bluff.

She said nothing, then watched Edgar spin around and stride out of the dining room before Tracy even realized what had happened.

What had she done?

She looked down at the now useless check and the paper that had set him off. David was`wrong. She shouldn't have pushed.

She wasn't going to cry.

But as she folded up the check and the agreement and slipped them both into her purse, she had to press her lips tightly together to hold back a vulnerable and unwelcome quiver. She had lost everything again.

Slipping her purse over her shoulder she dropped a couple of dollars on the table to cover her drink and a tip, then left the dining room.

As she entered the lobby, one of the double glass doors swung open and David entered, his eyes glancing around in the dimmer light. He wore a loose shirt over a T-shirt tucked into blue jeans, making him look younger than he did in his lab coat or coveralls.

The curious weightlessness that gripped her lately in his presence was offset by the loss she had just experienced. And she was suddenly angry.

He walked slowly over to her, his eyebrows lifted as if in question. "How did it go?" he asked, his voice quiet, his eyes holding hers.

"It didn't," she said flatly. "I pushed him, like you said I should. He went ballistic, and he left."

"What do you mean?"

"He walked out on me. Without my money and without signing that wonderful agreement you helped me put together," Tracy snapped, her anger and sorrow finding a focus in the man standing in front of her. She knew it wasn't his fault, but she couldn't stop. "I should have done as I intended. Make up nice and cozy to him and maybe he'd have my check and I'd have a piece of land."

David tunneled his hand through his hair. "He would have had your check and you'd have had no guarantees you would have gotten that land once he subdivided it."

"You don't know that." Tracy wrapped her hands around her purse, holding it close as if protecting the papers inside. "He promised me I'd get it."

"Tracy, you know that with someone like him a promise doesn't mean much without a signature on a piece of paper." David took a step closer. Touched her lightly on the shoulder, as if emphasizing his point. "You know even better than me what Edgar Stinson is like."

She did, but she also knew that right now Edgar Stinson held the only thing she had wanted, truly wanted, since she was young—a piece of land that represented the home she wanted to create for herself. The home her mother hadn't given her.

She looked up at David, aware that his hand still rested on her shoulder, large and warm.

"Well, thanks for stopping by," she said, taking a step back from him, her anger draining away, slowly being replaced by the all-too-familiar sorrow of loss. "I'm going home."

"Do you need a ride?"

She shook her head. Right now she didn't really want to spend time with David. Or anyone else. If she did, she was afraid she would take her first step into the pit of self-pity that lay at her feet.

She had spent enough time there.

Instead she gave him a quick nod farewell, then walked out the door and down the street to her apartment. She wished she could back up and get another shot at her time with Edgar Stinson. And this time she would just do what he wanted her to.

"My mommy says I can't keep the kitty," Kent said as he slowly reached his hand toward the cage. He touched the kitten carefully with one forefinger as if afraid to make too close a connection to the tiny animal.

The kitten lay curled up on its side, its head angled back, eyes closed, the poster kitty for feline contentment. It didn't even twitch when Kent stroked it down the side of its soft head.

After his mother's performance in the clinic yesterday morning Tracy had been positive she wouldn't see Kent for a long time. His mother must have gone out in order for Kent to dare to come back.

Kent shook his head and shoved his hands deep into the pockets of his worn jeans, almost pushing them off his skinny hips. "She just yelled at me and said no kitty and she means it."

Tracy's swift surge of anger surprised her both in its intensity and its speed. What would it hurt for this lonely little boy to have a kitten? A small companion to keep him company when he was alone. And she was sure that right now Kent knew Juanita wasn't coming home for a while, or else he wouldn't have dared come here.

"That's too bad. Maybe we can find someone else who can take care of it." Tracy tried to inject a cheerful tone into her voice that was as superficial as glitter on a cardboard angel's wings. Mixed with her anger was the practical reality of what she had done for this kitten. Thanks to her impulsive generosity, she was out a fair shot of money for a cat of dubious heritage and a questionable future.

There was no way she could take it, though she dearly would have loved to. If she had her own place...

Hold that thought. It's not happening.

She forced a smile to her lips, smothering the negative words before they overwhelmed her once again. God will make good His purpose for me, she thought, clinging to the love that had never left her since she'd discovered it as a young, lonely child.

"Would it help if I asked your mom if you could have the kitty?"

Kent shook his head so quickly his long, untidy hair flung out in an arc from his head. "You can't talk to her now. She went with Uncle Steve..." He pressed his lips together as if he had committed a grave breach of security.

Uncle Steve. The appellation rang a chorus of warning bells. "Uncle" indeed.

Kent glanced past Tracy, a brief expression of fear flitting over his face so quickly, Tracy thought for a moment "Uncle Steve" had come for him.

Tracy glanced over her shoulder and saw thankfully it was just Dr. Harvey. She pushed herself to her feet. "Hi, Alan. Kent and I were just trying to figure out who we should give his kitty to."

Dr. Harvey nodded, frowning at Kent, who now stood with his head bowed.

"We can put a notice up in the office. Someone will ask for it."

But Tracy didn't want just "someone" to get the kitten. She wanted a person who would let Kent come by once in awhile.

Crystal put her head in the doorway. "Tracy, Edgar Stinson to see you in reception."

Tracy couldn't stop the sudden surge of her heart, nor could she stop Kent from bolting away from her, his eyes still on Dr. Harvey. Then he spun around and ducked out the back door leading outside.

"Why's he so jumpy?"

"I think he's scared of men." And for a moment Tracy could identify with his fear. What would Edgar Stinson possibly have to say to her?

"I'll be in my office if Edgar needs to talk to me," Alan Harvey said with a wink. "Don't let him upset you."

He already had, Tracy thought. She wiped her suddenly sweaty palms down the sides of her lab coat, fluffed her hair and bit her lips. Then she sent up a quick prayer and walked out into the reception area.

Edgar stood with his back to the desk, his elbows resting on it, as if disdaining to look as though he was waiting. A small posture that didn't bode well for what Edgar might have to say.

Tracy glanced at Crystal who sat at the desk. Crystal lifted her hands in an I-don't-know gesture. No help there.

"Excuse me, Mr. Stinson, you asked to speak to me?"

Tracy said in what she hoped was an upbeat yet not groveling tone of voice.

Edgar spun around, his narrow eyes catching hers and once again holding her gaze in the same forthright and antagonistic way he had before.

And Tracy's heart started the same pounding it had before.

"I've come to talk about that land." He drummed his fingers restlessly on the counter. "You still got the check?"

"Yes. I have it." She swallowed down her exhilaration and dared even more. "And I still have the agreement."

His gaze held hers and Tracy didn't back down. Maybe David was right after all. Maybe he just needed someone to stand up to him.

The only sound in the office was the whispering tick of the clock, the clatter of keys from Crystal's keyboard and Dr. Harvey humming quietly in his office. The moment stretched, painfully long, and Tracy wondered who was going to give in this ridiculous, but high-stakes, game of chicken.

"Okay. I'll sign it," Edgar said, the first one to look away.

Tracy's knees almost gave out on her. "Great. I'll get the paper and the check." The two copies of the agreement were folded double and dog-eared from being shoved into her purse. But they were still legible.

She smoothed them out on the counter, handed Edgar a pen from the pocket of her smock. She held on to the check until he signed both copies above the signature she had so carefully scribed onto the paper yesterday.

"Thanks, Mr. Stinson," she said quietly, handing him the check and pushing one copy of the agreement toward him. "I'll keep my copy in a safe place."

Edgar held the check between his nicotine-stained fingers, then looked up at her, a crafty smile edging his lips. "I'm sure you will, missy. You play a good game." He tucked the check in the pocket of his worn, stained plaid coat and left the clinic without another word.

As soon as the door sighed shut behind him, Tracy let her shaky knees give way. She turned and slid to the floor and hugged her knees, elation and tears threatening at the same time. She had played hardball with Edgar Stinson and won the chance to dream again.

Crystal leaned back in her chair, grinning at her. "If I hadn't been here when that just happened, I don't know as I would have believed it."

"I can hardly believe it myself." Tracy closed her eyes and drew in a long, shuddering breath. "Thank you, Lord," she whispered, the adrenaline rush easing away, leaving her weak and wobbly. Excitement threaded with hope spun and whirled like a happy kaleidoscope. She slowly got to her feet as she tried to get her emotions settled.

"I better get back to ordering the supplies," Tracy said, heaving another sigh of relief.

Life was suddenly wonderful, she thought, almost floating back down the hall. All the plans she had discarded last night were now vibrantly alive and available again.

"What did Edgar Stinson want?" Dr. Harvey called out from his office.

Tracy leaned in the doorway, feeling as if she still could use a little support after the roller coaster of emotions she'd had to deal with the past couple of days. "Edgar Stinson just agreed to sell me an acreage."

Alan Harvey looked up at her over his glasses, marking his place in his book with a large forefinger. "What acreage?"

"The one he's going to subdivide for me. It's an old yard site that still has the power supply and some old buildings." Tracy hugged herself, reliving the incredible moment when Edgar Stinson had agreed to sign the papers.

"I know the place. It needs a lot of work." Alan looked over his glasses at her. "I can't believe you got Edgar to part with it. He's a hard man to deal with."

Tracy thought back to their quiet confrontation now and yesterday. "I got some good advice from David."

"Okay, I need to know what you're saying about me in front of my back."

Tracy jumped and spun around to face David, who was grinning down at her, his now-familiar smile warming her heart.

"I got it," she said, enthusiasm and pleasure spiraling through her as she impulsively caught his hands in hers. "Thanks to you, I got it."

"That's great. Details?"

Tracy laughed with sheer pleasure. "After yesterday I thought I'd lost the land. But Edgar came this morning and agreed to sign the papers."

"Wonderful."

When he squeezed her hands, she suddenly realized with a flush of embarrassment what she had done. But

David didn't release her hands when she gently tugged on them, his full smile softening his features.

And when he gently ran his thumb over the backs of her fingers, a sense of breathless waiting engulfed her. Slowly, her breath eased out of her chest.

"I…I owe you an apology," she said softly, looking down at his large, warm hands still holding hers. "I was wrong to be angry with your yesterday."

She gently pulled her hands out of his grip, reluctant to let go, but knowing she should. Their boss was sitting in a room behind them, probably avidly watching the entire process.

"So, did he tell you when you'd get possession?"

"He said he'd let me know when it was subdivided."

"That's great, Tracy. I'm really happy for you."

She chanced another quick glance up, pleased to see him still looking at her. "Well, I have to go order supplies." Her heart kicking up another notch.

What happened to her plan to be careful? Wary?

It was merely the excitement of getting the property. That was all.

And if she told herself that enough times she'd believe it.

"I'll help you."

"Well, there's no need," Tracy said, moving away from him. This was definitely getting dangerous. And it was not part of the plan for her life. Men didn't figure in that plan at all. And David was a man.

A good man, but still a man.

The buzzer rang and with a careful smile his way, she turned to answer the call of another customer.

The long blond hair and the slim figure of the woman standing by the counter sent a familiar shot of dislike through Tracy. Looked as though God was giving Tracy another stab at forgiveness. Though Misty Bredo hadn't been the cause of her breakup with Art, she was forever connected to that particular betrayal.

Misty glanced at Tracy, then past her as if dismissing her. Tracy took a long slow breath, sent up a quick prayer for patience and love and truth and grace and smiled at the woman who wasn't even looking at her.

"May I help you?" It was a long stretch to politeness but Tracy was pleased that she at least sounded competent and in charge.

"I need to talk to Dr. Braun."

Tracy usually got annoyed when clients asked for Dr. Harvey instead of David. But Misty's request for David made her hackles rise. And with that came a flash of painful jealousy.

"It's about my horses," Misty added, glancing past Tracy as if already waiting for David to come. Misty drummed her perfectly manicured nails on the wood, her deep blue eyes glancing around the clinic, curiosity mixing with disdain. Her thick blond hair was swept up in the back. In the front, long wisps of bangs swept in chic disarray down her cheeks. Her soft suede shirt and pants looked casual, yet striking.

"I'll get him." But Misty didn't even look at her.

She found David quickly enough; he was restocking a calving kit. The smile he gave her when she spoke his name was a warm counterpoint to the jealousy that had chilled her just seconds ago. "Misty Bredo wants to talk to you," she said, gesturing over her shoulder with her thumb. "Her parents own a large PMU operation a couple miles south of town."

"I know Misty," he said in a tone that indicated that he knew more than her name. More jealousy flared in Tracy's heart.

He washed his hands then walked with Tracy to the front of the clinic. "I was thinking about Kent's kitten," David said. "I figured I could use a little company around my place. I'm renting an older house on an acreage so it should be okay. You can tell him next time he comes around."

"I haven't seen him for a couple of days. I'm a little worried. After her visit here the other day, I'm sure his mother's been keeping him on a tight rein."

"Well as long as he's being taken care of."

Tracy thought of "Uncle Steve" and shivered. "I hope he is."

She heard a faint sigh from the reception room and, with a guilty start, took a step away from David. "We better go. Misty awaits."

"Something she doesn't do well," David said with a wink.

Misty was looking at one of the posters on the wall when Tracy followed David into the room. She spun around, her eyes narrowed with impatience, her arms clasped tightly across her chest. But as soon as she saw David, her eyes softened, her arms lowered and her mouth curved into a beguiling smile.

"So what can I help you with?" David asked, his deep voice pleasant and welcoming. And Tracy was surprised at how a tight grip of angry jealousy grabbed her.

"It's my horse." Misty leaned on the counter and with a languid gesture, tucked a wisp of hair behind her ear.

Tracy tried not to roll her eyes. Tried to pay attention to what she was supposed to be working on.

"Dr. Harvey was at my place the other day and diagnosed my horse with strangles. I was wondering if you could come and see if my horse is doing okay?"

"Did you give the horse the live strep equine vaccine?" David asked.

Misty nodded.

"And has there been any change?"

Misty shrugged. "I'm not sure. He seems okay, but I'd really like for you to come by and check him out."

Tracy tried not to roll her eyes. *Can you say "obvious"?* she thought, forcing herself to pay attention to her own work. She had a history with Misty though the woman seemed unaware of her existence.

Misty leaned on the counter, bringing herself a little closer to David. "Will you have a chance to stop by the farm and check him over?"

"I would prefer to talk to Dr. Harvey about that," David said, glancing back at Tracy. "He would want to do the follow up, I'm sure."

"I called him and asked him if you could come. He didn't mind."

"I think I'm busy, actually. Tracy, tomorrow's schedule is pretty full, isn't it?" David held her eyes, giving her a warning glance, but Tracy didn't know what he was warning her about.

She checked the appointment book. "You'll be going past Bredo's tomorrow afternoon. On your way to Dillards to dehorn some cows." Tracy glanced at Misty. "I'll have to bill you for the visit, though." Now didn't that sound all professional. David would be so proud.

But David looked slightly annoyed.

"I'm not worried about the billing," Misty said, shrugging off Tracy's comment.

Tracy knew that. A visit from David was not going to break the Bredo family.

Misty gave David another smile. "I look forward to seeing you tomorrow," she said softly.

I bet you are, Tracy thought with another intense flash of jealousy.

Without a glance at Tracy, Misty turned and left.

David waited until the door fell shut behind her, then turned back to Tracy, shaking his head. "So, why didn't you help me out?"

"Pardon me?"

"When she asked if I was coming by her place, couldn't you read my body language?"

"Guess I'm illiterate," she said with a light shrug, finally realizing what that look of warning had meant. "I was supposed to…?"

"Tell me I was going to be on the other side of the county that day," David finished for her. He folded his arms and leaned against the counter. "Now I have to go check out a horse that doesn't need my expert opinion."

"Well, you can check out Misty while you're there."

"I'm not interested in checking her out. You should know that, Tracy."

The serious tone in his voice made her look up, catch his gaze. Hold it.

David pushed himself away from the counter and walked to her side. "I'm not interested in her at all." He looked back over his shoulder, as if checking to see if anyone was around, then hunkered down, getting on eye level with her. "In fact, I was hoping to catch you alone."

He was so close she easily caught the scent of soap from his hands. Saw the glint of stubble on his chin. Could lose herself once more in the soft, hazel eyes that looked up at her.

Lose.

She didn't know if she liked the word *or* the emotion.

To her dismay, she found her heart beating even harder when he gave her yet another smile.

"Why is that?" This wasn't her most intelligent moment. She could feel the tingle of awareness that fizzed between them like champagne. Though it had been years since she'd felt any kind of attraction to a man, she vividly recalled the shivers it had created.

And this was definitely a shiver moment.

"I was wondering if you were busy Friday night."

Tracy tipped her head to one side, studying him, a peculiar feeling of joy bubbling up in her. Did she dare? Was this wise?

And how long was she going to let Art determine her life? It was just a date. It would do her good to get out.

"I'm not busy," she said quietly.

"Great. I've got tickets to a play in Edmonton. Would you like to come?"

"Sure."

And it was as easy as that.

He gave her his now-familiar crooked smile, brushed his fingers over the back of her hand, and Tracy felt a rare moment of contentment.

He pushed himself up, winked at her, and then left.

Seeing Misty with David wasn't a test. But as she glanced back at his retreating figure, she felt as if a barrier she hadn't been aware she had erected had disappeared.

Chapter Six

"So, if we add up parts and labor, it looks to me like..."
Tracy tucked the phone under her cheek as she punched
the numbers into the calculator sitting on her kitchen
counter, hit Total and stifled a latent scream. "...I have
a genuine scrap-heap automobile on my hands."

"Well, I could fix all the things wrong with it, but the
body is way rusted. Better to put your money into another ride." Chip laughed lightly. "But that's the way it
is with cops and mechanics. Usually no good news."

Tracy leaned her elbows on the counter, staring at the
figure on the calculator. Even though it was lower than
the price of a new vehicle, there was no telling what else
could happen once all this work was done.

Which meant she would be pulling money out of her
acreage fund for another vehicle.

"So, do you know of any good vehicles for sale?"
She'd been walking back and forth to work for the past

week, which was okay. But once it got colder and the snow came, that would no longer be an option.

"Nope. Not right now. But if I latch on to somethin' I'll let you know."

"And what should I do about my old car?"

"I'll get it to the auto wreckers. Don't worry about it."

"Thanks, Chip. I think."

Chip laughed and hung up. Tracy lowered the phone to the cradle, mulling over her options.

She could head down the road to the car dealership she had walked past on the way to and from work. Every day she saw large banners screaming out the amazing deals available to her with no money down and no interest.

And payments every month for the next four years. Which was about three years and ten months too many as far as she was concerned.

She groaned, thinking of the cost no matter which way she went. She could hold out for a few more weeks. As long as the weather held.

Sooner or later she was going to need another vehicle. For now, she had other things on her mind. Hair. Dress. Shoes. How long had it been since she'd dressed up for a date?

Months? She had gone out very occasionally. Often an old friend who wanted to catch up. She would double up with Danielle making a foursome out of a friend of Anthony's. But a serious date that could have repercussions?

It's just a date, she reminded herself as she kicked her runners off and walked to the bathroom for a shower. Just a date. Just a date.

* * *

"Well, that was…um…" David raised his hand in a vague gesture as he glanced over at Tracy.

"Bizarre?" she said helpfully.

David laughed, then dodged a woman in a leopard-skin bodysuit and a faux fur shawl as they made their way through the crowded foyer of the theater. "I don't know about you, but I don't think I'll ever be ready for a second act of that. How about you?"

Tracy shook her head. The heat combined with the crowd and the heavy scent of perfumes was making her dizzy.

"Then let's not waste our time here," he said, catching her arm and ushering her through the crush of warm bodies filling the foyer of the theater.

Tracy caught snatches of conversation.

"…a study in esoteric relational paradigms…fabulous, just fabulous…meaningful in an abstract sense… can't wait for the second act."

She bit back a smile. They must have seen a different play than she had. The only thing she couldn't wait for was escape.

Then, thankfully, they saw the doors. Freedom beckoned.

Outside, David dropped his head back, drew in a long breath and started to laugh. "I am so sorry," he said, once he caught his breath. "I really thought it was going to be something we could understand."

"Well, it was esoteric, in the strictest sense of the word."

David gave her a quick frown and she laughed. "Just kidding," she said. "I heard someone say something like that as we were leaving. Thought I'd show my avant-garde side."

Tracy had squirmed through meaningless dialogue, embarrassingly bad poetry and swirls of color and sound that assaulted the senses and said nothing.

She had glanced at David once or twice, catching him hunched down in his seat, arms crossed over his chest. His angry frown had made her laugh.

"Even a chick flick would have been preferable to that…whatever it was." David shuddered.

"Movies we can do in Preston." Tracy shivered lightly. "It's not every day I get to watch women throwing colored water at men for the sake of art." She shivered.

"You look like you caught some of the water," David said, glancing down at her. "Are you cold?"

"I'm an optimist. I don't wear my fall jacket until after Thanksgiving in October. It's not supposed to be this cool this early in the year."

Then, to her surprise and pleasure, she felt David slip his arm over her shoulder. "Well, your foolishness is my gain," he said lightly. "I can't be a gentleman and offer you my coat, so my arm will have to do."

It did just fine, Tracy thought, letting him pull her to his side, even as she kept her arms folded over her stomach. But she felt safe. Protected. Something she hadn't felt in a long time.

"Do you know any coffee places around here?"

Tracy looked around the busy downtown avenue, getting her bearings. "There's a little coffee bar not far from here."

David tilted her a grin. "Sounds good to me."

A few minutes later they were perched on stools at a table so small it was impossible to avoid elbow and eye contact.

"So whatever brought you to Preston?" Tracy asked, carefully sipping her hot chocolate as her arm inadvertently brushed David's. "It's not what I'd call a happening town."

David shrugged, playing with the foam of his latte. "It was a chance to get into a partnership, which is really rare for someone my age, and I have friends who live in Kolvik."

"Who are they?"

"Emily and her family. The lady I was sitting with the other Sunday in church. She and her family used to live next door to my family when I was growing up in Grande Prairie." He gave her a quick smile. "I went out with Emily's sister for a few years."

"I notice a past tense to that. Which, considering the fact that you asked me out on a date, is probably a good thing."

David's smile turned melancholy. "Heather died of cancer."

Tracy felt her heart clench. A grieving boyfriend. Not a good thing. "I'm sorry to hear that," she said softly, concentrating on a particularly large bubble in her hot chocolate that was proving difficult to pop.

David caught her hand, twined his fingers around hers and the bubble was forgotten. "It was sad, but not what you think it was. I was going to break up with her before she was diagnosed."

Tracy looked up into his soft hazel eyes as he tightened his grip.

"I didn't, because it would seem callous," he continued. "So I stayed with her until she died. It was sad, but it was the sadness of losing a friend more than anything."

Tracy mentally scrambled trying to find something comforting to say. Not a grieving boyfriend then. And while part of her wondered why it mattered, the other part of her was relieved.

"How long ago did that happen?"

David shrugged. "Long enough that the sadness is kind of comfortable. Long enough that I've been ready to move on for some time now."

The promise in his words hung between them. Tracy smiled back at him. "Moving on is good," she said softly.

"So tell me about your life," he said, his fingers toying with hers as if trying to draw out her secrets. "I understand you've lived in Preston a long time."

"I did go to college here in the city, so I'm not a complete hick."

"Ah. An incomplete one then," David teased. "What made you stay in Preston? Parents? Family?"

"Friends. Danielle mostly. And the fact that I like it. It's my home."

"Do you have family in town?"

Her mother wasn't a topic she wanted to bring up with David. Not in this quiet place with his hand wrapped around hers and the promise of more to come in his voice and eyes. A promise she felt ready to deal with. "My mother wasn't around much." She stopped there.

David waited a moment, as if giving her a chance for further confidences, but her family stories were exhausted. "So that's it? Just a mother that wasn't around much?"

Tracy nodded, giving him a quick, tight smile. "That's it."

"Sounds mysterious."

"That's me. Miss Mysterious," she quipped.

"You are. A bit. Kind of intriguing. In a beguiling, puzzling sort of way."

"You make me sound way more complicated than I am," she said, smiling.

He laughed. "I just know that I see different sides to you every time I'm with you. Now, you're a dark femme fatale who drinks hot chocolate and is kind of flirting with me, but not quite."

"I don't flirt." She tried to pull her hand back, but he wouldn't let her.

"Not on purpose," he said with a quick grin. "But then I see you with Kent and you're all soft and mothery and I get to see another facet of the amazingly interesting Miss Mysterious."

She wasn't going to blush at his teasing. But in spite of her resolve, a faint flush warmed her shoulders and she looked up at him, surprised to see the serious expression on his face. She held his gaze and something warm and wonderful unfurled in a part of her she thought could never be touched again.

"I'm pretty ordinary."

"Tell me what ordinary is for you these days."

So she did. From there they moved on to Preston. They talked about plans, life. Faith. She discovered that he had a brother. That his father still lived in Grande Prairie. That his mother had died three years ago. That he still missed her.

She told him what she dared, couching her youth in vague terms, mostly dwelling on the happy times she'd spent at Danielle's place.

And through all the casual conversation, he kept holding her hand, toying with her fingers, his gaze holding hers as they both retreated and advanced in an age-old dance of getting to know you.

"So. Date. David. You tell him you love him yet?"

Tracy tucked the phone under her ear as she dumped some sugar into her coffee. "Busy now," she said in shorthand to Danielle, as she glanced around the coffee room. David was reading the newspaper and Dr. Harvey and Crystal were playing a game of crib. Monday morning and they were catching a few moments of peace before the day started. "You should have come to church."

"Well I'm going to be gone tonight, so I need to find out."

"Learn to live with disappointment."

This weekend had been a turning point with her and David. A sense of a deepening relationship swirled unspoken around both of them. She felt ready and at the same time, she hesitated, as if afraid to expect that it would turn out right.

"He's there, isn't he?"

Tracy glanced over at David at the same time he looked up at her. And winked. Which made her blush.

"Was it fun? Enlightening? Romantic? Smoochalicious?"

"Two out of four isn't bad." Her neck was growing

warmer. She had to end this conversation soon or David would figure out what she was talking about.

"Which two?"

"Impossible to translate."

"Keep me in suspense much? Did you sit in church together on Sunday?"

"No." David had been on call. "Look, Dani, I should get going."

"Why? You don't start for at least another ten minutes." Danielle chuckled. "Tomorrow night you have to give me all the gory details. Promise?"

"Promise."

"And don't let this chance slip out of your hands. He's a great guy and worth taking a risk on. I've told you before and I'll keep telling you until you follow my advice." And with a click, her friend was gone.

Tracy hung up the phone, but couldn't face David quite yet. Her conversation with Danielle had resurrected all the emotions of the weekend, the hovering expectation that she knew would bring them to the next step.

Was she ready?

Did she dare open herself up to potential pain and loss?

She went to the bathroom. Caught her bearings again. Splashed cold water on her cheeks. Looked at her flushed face in the mirror. Thought again of David's tenderness with her. His openness.

Worth taking a risk on. Danielle's words rang in her ears. In time with the phone.

She heard David's deep voice answer it. Then he was calling her name.

She came into the coffee room and he was holding the phone out to her, a curious expression on his face. "It's your mother."

Chapter Seven

Tracy held the phone a little too tightly as she turned her back on David, unease flaring up in her. Why had her mother called her here? Now?

"Hello, this is Tracy."

"Hello, my little girl."

The voice created a storm of feelings in her chest. Feelings of abandonment, of sorrow, neglect, yearning. Anger.

Ever since Danielle had told her Velma Harris had called, a part of her had been waiting for this moment. She should have been prepared. But her trembling hands betrayed the surprise she felt. And she couldn't help but wonder what David thought about her newly resurrected mother.

"Just a moment, Velma." Tracy set the phone down and glanced at Dr. Harvey. "May I take this in your office?" she asked.

He nodded, his glasses glinting in the overhead lights

as he pushed himself away from the table. "When you connect, I'll hang this phone up."

Without a second glance at David, she left.

"I've got it," she said quietly, as she settled into Dr. Harvey's cracked leather chair. She heard a reassuring click and, for the first time in almost three years, she and her mother were alone.

"Hello, Velma," Tracy said unable to keep the chill out of her voice. Part of her wanted to hang up the phone, to deny her mother even the most minimal of contact. "How are you?"

"I'm okay."

Even after all this time, just the sound of Velma's voice could still send her into an emotional tailspin. She drew in a long slow breath and willed her pounding heart to still.

"Danielle told me you're living in Kolvik now?" Tracy dropped into a chair, resting her elbows on the desk. *Please, Lord, help me get through this.*

"I moved here a few weeks ago. I'm not working yet," Velma continued. "But I'm gonna go for an interview on Friday." Another pause.

Tracy pressed her elbows harder against the desk, squeezed her eyes shut, waiting for the inevitable plea for money.

Don't do it. You've given her enough. You can't buy her love.

"I wanna see you, Tracy. I've missed you."

A cold wave of anger coursed through Tracy at the yearning note in her mother's voice. This was worse than money. No communication for almost three years and now Velma wanted to have a cozy visit. Just like a real mother and daughter. Which they weren't.

"I don't know," she hedged. "I'm really busy."

"I want you to come visit me some day."

I want.

Not one question about Tracy's wants. Not one question about her daughter's life.

Tracy massaged her forehead with her fingertips, as if trying to draw out an answer that showed her mother she had regained some control over her life. That made her sound mature and in charge.

"I'm not sure. This is kind of sudden." Okay, maybe not so in charge. Or firm. How easily Tracy slipped back into a defensive role around her mother.

"You gotta ask Art?"

And wasn't that the best example of why Tracy shouldn't go to visit Velma?

"Art and I haven't been going out since your visit to his parents' store."

Silence after that remark.

"I wanna see you, Tracy," Velma said, her voice growing unexpectedly softer. "I have lots to tell you."

"Like what?"

"Mistakes. Things I did wrong."

The unexpected admission brought an abrupt and unwelcome onrush of expectation. Her mother never admitted to making mistakes. She just made them.

"I want to make things right with you, Tracy. Can you come?"

"Will you be around if I make plans?" Tracy resented the longing she heard in her own voice. Resented the old need her mother easily resurrected. Whatever happened to putting the past behind her? Getting on with her life? How could she do that when it kept sneaking up on her like this?

"I promise."

"Don't promise, Velma. Do."

"I will. I want you to come. Can you come this Sunday?"

"I don't know. I don't have a car that works." The excuse was a flimsy defense. If Danielle caught even a whiff of this conversation she would offer her car before Tracy could find a reason to deny the offer.

"Someone can drive you, can't they? One of your friends? Danielle's brothers?"

Tracy was surprised that her mother even remembered Danielle. Or that she had brothers.

"Can't someone bring you?" Velma asked. "I really need to see you."

It was the pleading note in her mother's voice that sideslipped Tracy to a place she'd pledged she'd never go again.

"Maybe I can find someone. I'm not going to make any promises." She left herself open, unwilling, unable to make more than a cursory plan. "Give me your number and I'll let you know if I come." She scribbled the number down and looked at it as if by writing it she had already made a commitment.

"Call me," Velma said. "I'll be waiting."

Tracy waited a moment, then hung up. She closed her eyes, resting her head on her hands.

I'll be waiting.

That was her line, not her mother's.

Tracy had spent most of her childhood waiting. Waiting for her mother to come home from her job at the pub. Waiting for her mother to wake up. Waiting for her mother to fulfill any one of the many promises she threw at Tracy whenever guilt overtook her.

Unbidden came memories of herself at age twelve, sitting on a couch in an empty apartment. She and her mother had just moved to Preston. Her mother had been full of promises that this place would be good. That things would be different.

And they were. For the first few weeks.

Then her mother started coming home from work later, leaving Tracy alone most evenings. Always the worst time.

One such evening, Tracy was watching television, eating a bowl of cereal. After doing her homework, she had fallen asleep on the couch. At two o'clock, Tracy had woke up in a panic. Afraid and alone, she had rushed to her mother's bedroom. The bed was empty. Tracy crawled into her own bed and twenty minutes later her mother came stumbling in.

The next morning her mother acted as if nothing had happened. When Tracy asked her where she'd been, Velma merely shrugged. Just out. Phoning was an inconvenience.

An inconvenience that happened before and would happen many times after. No explanations, no communication to tell a frightened young girl where her mother was.

Those were the bad times.

The good times were when her mother cheered up. Put on makeup. Took Tracy out shopping and out for supper. Her mother would be a laughing companion and Tracy would forget the dark hard times, thinking that this time they had turned a corner. That her mother was going to make the changes she promised she would make.

But in Preston the good times grew further apart, the dark times more frequent. Sometimes Tracy couldn't stand it anymore, and she would leave the empty apartment, walk the streets.

On one such night, six months after Velma and Tracy had moved to Preston, Tracy, alone and bored, had wandered farther than usual. She'd ended up in front of a brightly lit church six blocks from their apartment. As the people spilled out she recognized a girl from school. Danielle.

Luckily for Tracy, the message that evening had been about befriending strangers. Right then and there Danielle decided to apply the sermon and Tracy found a better place in her life. Danielle invited her over. It was Alice, Danielle's mother, who had encouraged Tracy to come as often as she wanted. When she was older Tracy had often wondered if Alice knew what Tracy's home life really was like.

Not that anyone found out from Tracy herself. Shame and fear kept the truth locked away. In the town where they had lived before, Tracy had tried to tell her teacher about her mother's drinking spells but the teacher hadn't believed her. Nor had the neighbor lady who asked why Tracy was so often alone. So, in this new place she said nothing, hiding her shame, treasuring Danielle's friendship and the times she could spend at her place.

When Tracy had moved to Edmonton after high

school to take her vet tech course on Dr. Harvey's encouragement, Velma must have considered her "mothering" duties done, and she'd left Preston, returning only periodically.

A year after she'd started school, Tracy met Art at a party thrown by friends of Danielle's parents. Art and his parents had just bought into a business in Preston. Tracy was enchanted by his charm and his attention.

They'd started dating, making plans. As soon as she graduated, Dr. Harvey offered her a job, and she'd snapped it up, anxious to be back in Preston and closer to Art.

When Danielle had opted to come back to Preston, Tracy thought her life had reached a measure of fullness that was her due after years of sorrow and want.

The only sour note were the mothers: Art's and her own.

Her mother came to visit sporadically, stopping in unexpectedly and usually when it was most inconvenient. Usually unkempt and drunk. Usually broke and usually asking for money. Tracy had tried to be firm, but each time her mother came, Tracy nurtured a faint hope that this time things would be different. This time the good mother, the one that grew more faint with time, would be the mother who would show up on her doorstep.

It never was.

Art's mother wouldn't stop by at all. In fact, for the most part Janice Vermeer preferred to act as if Tracy was invisible. She made no secret of her dislike of Tracy. Oh, she would be very polite in front of Art, but the real Janice showed when Art was gone.

Then came the fateful day when Velma had come to

Janice and Lance's clothing store. She had mouthed off at Janice and made loud, disparaging comments about the selection. Of course, she'd been drinking.

Then, after trying on a number of dresses and shirts, insulting Art, swearing at his parents, she had left the store. Janice let Tracy know, in no uncertain terms, that Tracy and her mother would never have a place in Art's family. Shortly after that Art stopped calling. When Tracy found out he had taken Misty Bredo out, she knew it was over. Janice thought it was for the best and Art must have thought so, too.

And whenever Velma came to town, Tracy would hear again Janice's voice telling Tracy she wasn't good enough for her son.

Tracy dragged her hands over her face, pressing her fingers into her skin as if to hold herself together. She didn't want her mother in her life anymore. She had her own plans. Her own life.

She pushed herself away from the desk, restlessness edging her movements. She wanted to run. To leave.

Which wasn't going to happen. In five minutes she and David were heading to Devlins' purebred Angus farm to give blackleg boosters to their steers and heifers. After that they had to go do some more preg testing at Plantingas'. Which meant they would be spending most of the morning together.

And when she stepped out of Dr. Harvey's office, David was there, filling the hallway with his presence. His eyes held hers, a puzzled frown wrinkling his forehead.

"So that was your mother."

Tracy's gaze skittered over his. "Yes, that was Mom."

He laughed lightly, a humorless sound. "I thought she was dead."

"Sorry. She's not." She gave him a careful smile. "Sorry if I misled you."

He said nothing and Tracy wished it didn't matter so much.

The quiet drive to Devlins' farm only added to her discomfort. But she kept her eyes on the fields flashing past the window and her lips clamped together. This was not the time in their relationship, such as it was, for confidences about her mother.

When they got to Devlins' the steers and heifers were already penned up, separated from their bawling mothers, which meant they could start right away.

"Thanks for coming out." Marnie Devlin yelled above the non-stop noise of the cattle. "We usually do this ourselves, but..." She patted her bulging stomach and nodded her head toward her husband, Justin, who was climbing awkwardly over the corral fence, his arm in a sling.

"Glad to help," David called out. "How many head?"

"One hundred and twenty."

An all-morning job, thought Tracy, setting out the vials and syringes on a makeshift table Marnie had sitting by the headgate.

The noise made conversation impossible, a small blessing. The silence on the drive up here had been difficult enough to endure.

As Tracy watched Marnie and Justin work their cows, she envied their ease with each other. The lack of shouting and barely discernible hand motions easily showed their rapport with each other and with their animals. And when she caught David watching them, a wistful smile on his face, she wondered if he felt the same.

In spite of the noise of the concerned cows, the rhythm of the work and the steady movement of animals all soothed Tracy's jangled nerves. And the occasional smile David sent her way was like a gentle benediction that gave her hope that she was forgiven.

When the gate clanged shut for the last time, the last heifer ran to freedom and the once-irate cows herded their young away from the yard, into the bare pasture beyond the corrals. The only sign of their presence was a slowly settling cloud of dust.

"That went well," Justin said, checking the gate. "Thanks so much for coming."

"No problem." David stripped off his gloves and threw them in the box holding the empty vials. "When do you figure on weaning and shipping them?"

Justin waggled one shoulder. "I'm waiting for the price to head up a bit before we do that."

"Just send the bill in the mail," Marnie said. She rubbed her stomach and glanced at Justin. "And, well, we were wondering…"

Here it comes, thought Tracy.

"Would we be able to pay half of the bill now and half in a couple of months?" Marnie asked.

She released her breath in a sigh and caught an unexpected wink from David.

"That should be okay," he said. "Tracy can make a note of it on your file."

Their thanks were effusive, and, as David and Tracy left the yard, they stood in the driveway, waving them off like expected company.

"Jobs like that are always nice," David said quietly as he pulled out of the driveway onto the gravel road. "Though I do feel as if I was taking advantage of a bad situation."

"That's how Dr. Harvey got into the medicine-discounting business," Tracy said, clicking her seat belt shut, thankful for the ordinariness of shop talk. "Unfortunately he usually cut the deals for the hard-nosed businessmen, the ones who could afford to pay full price and had enough moxy to ask."

"I'm tempted to give this couple a break," David said, tapping his fingers on his steering wheel. "Though where does that stop?"

"One advantage of owning your own business," Tracy said. "You make that call."

David threw her a smile. "What would you do?"

She was encouraged by the smile. And by his request for advice. "Not charge interest on the unpaid balance for a month. But that's all. It's not like you're raking in the bucks."

"And you would know, Miss Bookkeeper."

His light banter soothed her previous nervousness. "I would know."

He slowed for a corner and Tracy sat up, craning her head. Her future acreage lay down the road, in the other direction.

"See something?"

"It's just…" She faltered, her innate caution holding

her back. But she had held back enough, she realized. "My future new place is just half a mile down this road." Tracy's heart gave a little skip as she pointed out the row of spruce and poplar trees that had once formed the shelterbelt for the old farmstead.

David bent over to see better then turned and drove toward it.

The driveway was narrow, edged by overgrown aspen and pine trees, giving the lane a secluded and secretive look. Tracy leaned forward as they rounded the last curve and turned into the yard.

A wooden granary, gray and weatherbeaten, tilted toward the old hip-roof barn that held traces of once-red paint. Willows bristled around its foundations, like the whiskers of an old, unkempt man. But in spite of age and time, the barn still stood. Solid and unbent.

"This place has potential," David said, putting the truck in Park.

"Potential to make me broke and crazy, according to Danielle." Tracy got out of the truck and looked around, glad that David had turned the truck off. She closed her eyes and listened. The only noise wafting across a stillness was the tick tick of the truck engine cooling off, the soft sigh of a light breeze waving the dry grass.

Silence. Blissful, blessed silence.

She waded through the tangled grass to the small square of concrete, all that was left of the old house. A few hardy peony bushes hugged the foundation, their leaves still green in spite of the frosts.

"What happened here?" David asked, easily catching up to her, his hands tucked into the front pockets of his blue jeans.

"A tragic story apparently. The husband had been working in the bush for the winter to make some extra money and the wife had overloaded the woodstove. She barely got out with the kids. The family went broke and Stinson bought the place." She glanced around the remains of the house, a sad smile edging her lips. "Some say she burnt the house down on purpose because she was so depressed."

"What do you say?"

"I say it doesn't matter. I'm putting my house here. I'll make new stories. Better ones." Tracy stepped inside the foundation as if claiming ownership right then and there. She hugged herself, unable to stop the smile that tugged at her lips and sang through her heart. Her own place. "I'm going to have windows on every wall so I can see the sunrise, feel the warmth of the sun in the middle of the day and see the sunset in the evening."

"And out of the north windows?"

"The northern lights, of course."

David stepped inside the foundation and Tracy watched him come toward her. Watched how his shoulders shifted with each step. How the breeze toyed with the hair that hung over his forehead.

And where did he fit in her dream world?

"Come and have a look at the barn." When she reached the heavy wooden door, David was right behind her. She grabbed the handle and tugged but the door didn't give.

David stepped in to help and when he pulled, the door

gave reluctantly with a painful screech of metal on metal. "You'll need to oil that."

"I need to do a lot of things, I'm sure." Tracy stepped into the musty interior of the barn, her feet tapping lightly on the dusty wooden floor. "Over there is a stall I could use for a milk cow. Another plan from another time. But behind us," she half turned, pointing to a pen, "a place for chickens. Less maintenance than a cow and I'll probably be able to keep up with their production. I could stable some horses. There are great places for riding around here." She glanced back at David, but his hooded gaze was on her, not the wooden partition she was pointing out.

She lowered her hand, her eyes snared and caught by his. In the faint gloom of the barn, his strong features were shadowed, mysterious and beguiling.

He took a slow step nearer, his hands still in his pocket. "So this is your future."

"With prayers and hard work, I hope it's a future that's better than my past." The words slipped out and once spoken, hung between them. The barest hint of what had come before.

"A past that includes your mother?"

"Yes, my mother." Tracy turned to him, digging for the right words to explain why she had misled him.

"I'm guessing it's been some time since you've heard from her?"

"Three years. I thought she had disappeared from my life."

"Where is she now?"

"Kolvik. Forty-five minutes away." Tracy hugged herself, still unable to reconcile her mother's return.

"Why did you let me think she was dead?"

Why wouldn't he leave this alone? Tracy shrugged his question away. Countered with, "She wants me to come and visit."

"Are you going to?" He took the evasion.

"Well, for once I'm glad that my car is on the fritz. I have no way of getting to Kolvik."

David covered her hand with his. "I'm going to Kolvik on Sunday. If you want, I could give you a ride."

Tracy felt pushed into places she didn't want to go. "I'm not sure I want to."

"At the risk of sounding as though I'm interfering, I think you should go."

"And why do you think that?"

"I always sensed some sadness when you talked about your mother. At first I thought it was because she was dead. But I wonder if it isn't something else."

"Please, don't read more into my tone of voice than is there." She didn't mean to sound sharp, but she didn't like the idea that David thought her mother's silence in her life had made her sad. "Anyway, if I wait, she'll probably disappear. She always has."

"Then wouldn't it be even more important to connect with her? What if you regret not going?"

Tracy held his sincere gaze, listening to his words but hearing beneath them a gentle reprimand and expectation. And at the same time she realized that he couldn't know. Couldn't understand her life.

"Why do you care?" she asked.

"Because for some reason I have been struggling to understand, you matter to me."

"I'm hard to understand?" His statement was like a back-handed compliment.

"You are. You hold back and you don't say much, yet when I see you with Kent I see a glimpse of a woman who can care deeply, but is afraid of something. I wish you weren't afraid," he said.

His quiet words had snared her, stole coherent thought.

"I don't want to be," she whispered, the words drawn out of her, past her fragile defenses.

David smiled, then cupped his hand around her chin, lowered his head to hers and gently kissed her.

A deep inexpressible yearning flared up at the touch of his lips on hers. He pressed his lips to her cheek, then her forehead as he drew her close.

"I've wanted to do this for a while," he whispered, his hand tangling in her hair. "I'm not great with words."

"You don't have to talk." She slipped her arms around him, holding him close, feeling once again safe and protected in the haven his arms created.

He gently fingered her hair back from her eyes. He smiled down at her. "I'm sorry if I sounded like I was lecturing you about your mother. I just…" He paused, his eyes following the track of his finger. "It's just that I can't stop thinking about my brother and our mother."

"I thought your mother was dead."

"And that's the problem. She and my brother fought. When she died unexpectedly they never had a chance to reconcile. He's been sorry ever since." He smiled carefully down on her. "Family is so important. Mothers are so important. I'm just thinking of you. I'll come with you if you want."

She didn't want. For all his talk of reconciliation, she knew for a fact she wanted to keep her mother and David as far apart as she could. But this much she could do for him. In spite of her misgivings, she wanted to gain his approval.

"I'll go with you on Sunday." She didn't know if it would change anything, but for David's sake she knew she had to try.

His smile showed her she had done the right thing. And now it was time to move away from her past.

"So that's the barn," she said taking a step away from him. "We don't have time to see much else…"

His thumb lightly caressed her cheek. "We can save that for another day."

The faint promise of those words sang between them. "I suppose we should be going."

He didn't touch her again, but he didn't have to. As they walked back to the truck she was aware of his every move.

The drive back to the clinic was so quiet, Tracy couldn't help wondering if that moment of closeness had never happened. But when David parked the truck in the lot behind the clinic, his smile reminded her.

The back door of the clinic burst open and Crystal ran out, waving at him to come inside.

"We've got an emergency," she called as they got out of the truck. "Dog run over. I need you stat."

Crystal and David ran back into the clinic and while they got ready, Tracy returned to the front desk and a distraught owner.

David's kiss was pushed to the back of her mind.

But not forgotten.

Chapter Eight

Tracy shivered as she slipped the key into the door of the vet clinic. This walking to work was growing old and tired. It was bad enough during the week, but somehow it was worse on Saturdays when all she had to do was check up on and feed the animals. This meant she had to walk for half an hour to do fifteen minutes of work. Sooner or later she'd need to break down and buy a car. At least David had a vehicle. Tonight he was going to pick her up and take her to a movie.

The thought of another date with David put a smile on her face. She dared let herself make a few plans. Dream a few extra dreams.

She hung up her coat, rolled up her shirtsleeves and walked down the hallway whistling a tuneless song, stopping when she saw the kennel-room door ajar. She heard a sudden scrambling inside.

She pushed the door wide just as Kent got the back door open.

"Kent. It's okay. It's me. Tracy." She pitched her voice low and quiet, quelling the urge to run across the room and grab him. Hold him tight.

The morning light angled into the room, casting the boy's face in shadows as he turned slowly to her.

"You're not mad?"

"Of course not, sport." She stayed where she was, recognizing too well his ready-to-run stance. "How did you get in?"

He ducked his head again, fidgeting with the hem of his T-shirt. "I…I…came in yesterday. Then I hided."

Why hadn't he come to her? Why hadn't he told her he needed help? Her heart twisted at the thought that he had spent the night alone here. Again.

And where was his mother?

She tamped her anger. Kent looked scared and alone, and she had to reassure him. Who knows what his mother had told him? Tracy crouched down, bringing herself on eye level with him.

"Are you hungry, Kent?"

He dug his finger deeper into the hole, stretching it. "Mom says I'm not allowed to let you feed me."

"How about we go talk to your mommy about that?" Because Tracy was pretty positive that if Kent had spent the night here, his mother was gone. So Tracy could, in theory, take Kent anywhere.

Kent pulled his mouth in, considering, then nodded.

"We can go once I've taken care of the animals." It broke her heart to think that his own kitten was getting fed and cared for better than he seemed to be.

When they were done she helped him wash his hands

and convinced him to wash his dusty face as well. The clothes she could do nothing about.

"There you go, sport," she said, fingering a lock of hair out of his eyes. "All spit and polished."

As he smiled up at her, a peculiar sensation curled through her midsection. She wanted to pick him up. Tuck his head into her neck and hold him close. Protect him.

"Let's go, then," she said, holding out her hand. And to her amazement and wonder, he took her hand and held tight.

After checking out Kent's place and seeing that his mother wasn't home after all, Tracy took him directly downtown and picked up some clothes for him. He balked initially until she told him that she hadn't had a chance to get him a birthday present. Thankfully the ruse worked.

As soon as she got him to her apartment, she gave him a bath and dressed him in his new clothes.

And then she phoned Danielle.

"I did some asking around the past couple of days," Danielle said. "All I know is that the neighbors said they heard a lot of fighting, worse than usual apparently on Thursday night and haven't seen anyone since."

Tracy pressed her anger back. Kent was here now. He was safe.

"So what do we do?" She was holed up in her bedroom, away from Kent who was happily playing in the living room with some bricks they had bought. "What about his family?"

"My next step is to check with the hospitals and the police," Danielle continued. "See if she ended up there.

But for now, Kent is safe and as far as I'm concerned he's your first priority."

"We're going to help him, aren't we, Danielle? He's not going to fall between the cracks, is he?"

"I can't make any promises, Tracy, you know that. If his mother comes back and takes Kent there's nothing we can do to stop her. Not right now."

Tracy clutched the phone so hard her fingers ached. "I gave him a bath just a few moments ago, Danielle. He's got some bruises. Old and new. A couple on his chest. One fresh, one slightly yellow. Three on his back. All older. A set of fingerprints on his upper arm." She stopped as her anger surged once again. "So what do we do?"

"Keep looking for the mother. If she doesn't show up in the next couple of days, we can declare him abandoned and I can apply for temporary guardianship."

"Okay. I'll keep phoning the apartment. All I get is the answering machine, though."

"I'll stop by the place tonight again before I head to the theater."

"And I'm going to be busy on Sunday as well."

"Really. Why?"

"Not what you think. My mom called. She wants me to come visit."

Danielle's silence showed Tracy how much her friend understood.

"You going?"

"Yes. David is taking me. He has something going on in Kolvik as well."

"That's nice. I think."

"The David part is nice."

"I think it's good you're going, Tracy. The way your mom was talking…"

She didn't need to hear anyone else defend her mother. "Well, I'm doing it as much because David encouraged me to as anything. I don't want him to think I'm some unforgiving harpy."

"You're not that, Tracy. But I do think it's good that you're going—for your sake. Did you make sure she's going to be home?"

Tracy bit her lip, resenting the brush of guilt she felt at Danielle's light probing. "She's the one who contacted me wanting a visit. I shouldn't have to go chasing her down. If she can't remember that, well then I don't know if…"

"It's okay, Tracy. I was just being a friend."

"I'm sorry. I'm a little keyed up about it, is all."

"It will be fine."

Tracy doubted that but appreciated Danielle's reassurances. "As soon as you hear anything about Kent's mom, can you call me?"

"You'll be first on my list. Take care."

Tracy disconnected and sank down on the bed, her emotions veering between nervousness over her visit with her mother and anger with Kent's mom.

Pictures of her own childhood flashed with searing intensity into her mind. The fear and the uncertainty of waiting.

Tracy pressed her clenched fists against her mouth as if holding back the memories. She had to stay on top of them.

"I need your help, Lord," she whispered, against her

hands. "This little boy's story is too much like my own. Too close. Too close." She rocked a moment, losing herself in her prayer, in God's strength. As she reminded herself again and again, God's love would hold her up.

"Look what I made." Kent burst into her room, yanking Tracy out of the moment.

He was waving an airplane made out of bricks, his lips vibrating with little-boy spitting noises that she presumed were supposed to be the sound of the plane's engines. In spite of her anxiety, his exuberance and happiness pulled an answering response from her.

They spent the next hour sprawled out on the living-room floor following the instructions for a car and a boat and another airplane.

When they had exhausted all the possibilities of the bricks, Tracy and Kent walked to the library and took out some books and videos.

While Kent watched one of the movies, Tracy tried to phone his home one more time. Still no answer.

She looked up her mother's number, then picked up the phone, her finger hovering over the buttons. Should she? Shouldn't she?

Was this a test? Before she could make up her mind, the phone rang in her hand, making her jump.

A quick glance at call display showed her who it was.

And her heart started up again. It was David.

"Hello, David," she said, turning her back to Kent, before she even realized what she was doing. Like a teenage girl hiding her secret boyfriend from her mother.

"Hey, there. How are you doing?"

"I'm good. Kent is here."

"What? How did that happen?"

Tracy cupped her hand over the handset, walking down the hall. "I found him this morning in the clinic again. I've been trying to phone his mother all day, but there's no answer. Danielle has been trying to track her down as well."

David's silence underlined her own concern. "This is the second time. What happens now?"

"Danielle is taking care of things for now. He's okay here."

"I'm guessing the movie is off for tonight, as is coming over."

"He's a little jumpy yet. So I guess we'll see you tomorrow at church. Danielle will be picking me up." Tracy felt a flutter of anticipation mixed with the thought of seeing her mother.

"I'll see you tomorrow, then," David said.

Tomorrow. She liked the sound of that.

Chapter Nine

"What is this place?" Kent asked as Danielle pulled into the half-full parking lot. "I never been here before."

"This is a church," Tracy said, turning back to Kent, who sat hunched in the back seat, his hands pressed under his legs. His hair was neatly combed. His new shirt held starched peaks and valleys. The corduroy pants he wore still had that fresh-from-the-store sheen. "This is where we're going to be this morning."

Kent frowned, as he ran his thumb up and down the seatbelt across his chest. "Is this a good place?"

Tracy smiled. "It's a very good place," she said quietly. "One of the best places you can be."

As they walked toward the church, Kent clung to Tracy's hand, walking beside her, ignoring Danielle, who gently tried to engage him in conversation. He replied in monosyllabic answers, as if he sensed what she was—a dreaded social worker.

Danielle threw Tracy a questioning look, but Tracy

knew far better what Kent was dealing with than Danielle, in spite of all her training and experience, could ever know or understand.

She clung just a little tighter to Kent's hand, surprised by a wave of feelings she could only describe as maternal.

This little boy needed a home. Stability. If his mom didn't show up soon, he was going to end up in the system.

And in a foster home.

I could take him in, she thought.

The idea came with a soft slide into her mind, but as she tested it, as she glanced down at Kent's dark head so close to her hip, she knew it was right. She could be a mother to this little boy. Who better to understand what he needed? What he wanted?

It was too early to make any decision. To make any plans. But the longer Kent's mother stayed away, the bigger the chances were that this little boy was going to end up in care.

And she wanted to be as involved as she could in his life.

I can do this, Lord, she thought, clinging to Kent's hand. Relishing the feel of his warm fingers wrapped around hers. *With Your help, I can take care of this child.*

And what about his family?

What if they suddenly appeared out of the woodwork?

Danielle had told her enough stories about long-lost grandparents, aunts and uncles mysteriously showing up at court cases, suddenly keenly interested in the well-being of a child they had had little or nothing to do with before. She had long suspected these eleventh-hour appearances were more a desperate bid to keep the child out of the hands of Child Welfare than true concern for the child.

And if that happened with Kent, Danielle would have to weigh their suitability against hers. Family often held greater sway in child welfare cases than an interested third party. Kent might slip into the system and she might never see him again.

Enough. Enough.

Tracy pushed back the flurry of worried voices. She had a job to do and however God saw fit to use her in this child's life, she would have to abide with that.

The church was half full by the time they got into the sanctuary. Danielle and Tracy went to their usual spot behind Danielle's father.

Arnold flashed a quick smile at Tracy as he turned around. "Hey, girl. How are ya?"

"Good, thanks. Busy at work."

"Who's the kid?" Arnold's booming voice was toned down in deference to the fact that he was in church. Barely.

Tracy tried not to wince as she glanced at Kent, gauging his reaction. "This is Kent. Kent, this is Danielle's dad, Mr. Hemstead." Kent ducked closer to Tracy, not even raising his eyes as she made the introduction. No surprise.

Had Danielle's mom been alive, Tracy knew that Alice would have reached in her purse and given the boy one of her never-ending supply of candies.

There were many times she missed Alice even more

than she missed her own mother. And if Alice was still alive, Tracy would have been at her home in a heartbeat, asking advice on what to do about her own mother.

"He's a little shy," Tracy murmured, squeezing Kent's hand, hoping Arnold would get the hint.

"I'm not a shy," Kent mumbled, still looking down. "I'm a boy."

"And a big boy," Arnold said, managing to restrain his usually boisterous self. "So how's things with the new boyfriend, Tracy?"

Tracy gave her friend a pained look, but Danielle was ignoring her, as if to say, "I live with this all the time. Get over it."

Tracy looked back at Arnold, held his gray eyes with her own direct gaze. "What boyfriend?"

"Nice try, girlie," he said with another grin. "I saw you sitting with him a few Sundays ago. Heard you went to a play. I'll be expecting to see an announcement in the bulletin soon."

Tracy gave him a weak smile, unable to think of anything fast enough.

"Is this seat taken?"

The deep voice above her startled Tracy, and, as she looked up, her heart fluttered in her rib cage like a captured bird. David stood at the end of the pew, one hand tucked into the pocket of black dress pants. His loose-knit cream cotton sweater gave him a casually dressy look. But it was his half smile that gave an extra hitch to Tracy's breath.

"No. You can sit here if you like." She unconsciously moved aside, as if there wasn't enough room.

"Hey, there, David," Arnold said, still half twisted in his seat, watching Tracy closely.

Tracy dragged her gaze away from him, as politeness and duty overran her natural instinct to duck. To hide. She hoped, prayed that David hadn't heard Arnold's teasing.

"Arnold Hemstead, this is David Braun. I'm sure you've met him before. David this is Arnold, Danielle's father."

David reached across Tracy to shake Arnold's hand. "How is your horse?"

"Good, now. Never did see such a bad case of laminitis. It'll be a while, but that farrier you recommended seems to know his stuff."

"Glad to hear it."

Another older man dropped into the pew beside Arnold and thankfully Tracy saw him get caught up in conversation about the harvest and crop yield.

David's gaze skimmed Tracy's again as he returned his attention to Kent. "I'm going to be taking care of your kitty," he told Kent, resting his elbows on his knees. "If you want, you can come and visit him."

Kent glanced up, suddenly interested. "Can Tracy come and visit too?"

David's slow smile crawled across his lips. "I hope she does."

The comment dangled between them. Her feelings for David were so tender, so new, she didn't dare invest too much hope in them. If David met Velma, she was afraid the fragile connection that held them now would be shattered, as had the connection with Art.

The church service started and Tracy sat back, smiling down at Kent who was still busy with his paper. This little boy she understood. He needed her and he was safe. She gently feathered a long strand of hair away from his forehead and he glanced up at her with a quick grin.

Such a little thing. But it flew straight to Tracy's heart and burrowed deep.

Then she chanced a look at David who was watching her with a bemused expression. She tilted a careful smile in his direction.

And when he smiled back, it was as if something precious took root.

"She's not home." Kent trudged out of his apartment, giving one more quick glance over his shoulder, as if hoping he would be surprised. "I looked and looked." He gave a little sniff.

Tracy hunkered down and drew him close to her, comforting him. "Do you know where she would go?"

"Maybe with Uncle Steve."

"Do you know Uncle Steve's last name, Kent?" she asked, tenderly wiping the tear from his cheek. Maybe if they knew at least that.

Kent glanced up at her, and then away. "Stinson," he mumbled.

Tracy's heart plunged. Of all the names to have.

"But I don't want to go to Uncle Steve's place. He's mean. He hurts me."

Tracy bit down her anger as she slowly got to her feet. "I guess I won't be coming with you, David," she said quietly. "I'll have to take care of Kent." She couldn't imagine taking this poor broken little boy to her mother's place. Going to see her mother was a survival situation. She would need all her defenses in place and Kent would need too much individual care.

"He can spend the day with me," David said, reaching down and clasping Kent by the shoulder. "What do you say, sport? Do you mind spending some time with me and my family?"

Kent nodded and sniffed once more. "Can Tracy come?"

"Tracy has to visit her mommy. But she can ride with us."

"I don't need to see my mother today. I can do that anytime." If she talked long enough she could convince herself that this was the best course.

David's sad smile slipped behind her feeble protests. "She'll be disappointed."

Tracy almost laughed. "I doubt that."

She didn't like how his smile faded away to a disapproving frown.

David opened the door of the truck and let Kent scramble into the back seat. "I know you don't think it's necessary, but she's your mother after all."

"After all…" Tracy stopped, remembering too well the "all" of life with Velma.

"Emily's family would enjoy having Kent visit. They're used to people coming and going." He buckled Kent in and pushed the front seat back, resting his elbow on it as he faced Tracy. "Emily's mom and dad have been foster parents for years. Emily and her husband have done it as well."

Heather's perfect family.

The opposite of hers.

The little, poisonous thought floated like a whiff of acrid smoke across her mind, and with a shake she dispersed it. Tracy hadn't chosen her mother, but she had chosen how she was going to live her life.

And she had nothing to be ashamed of. If she said it long enough, maybe she would start to believe it.

"If that's okay with them, then, I suppose we should get going." She didn't like the snippy tone of her voice. Her defense mechanism was too finely tuned these days.

She moved to get into the truck, but David's hand on her shoulder stopped her.

"I wasn't trying to be the missing father figure in your life." The light touch of humor in his deep voice, coupled with a half smile, softened the stiffness of her spine. Melted her resistance.

"I'm sorry, too. I'm just feeling a little tense."

David's hand tightened on her shoulder as he helped her into her seat.

Five minutes later, David turned onto the highway leading to Kolvik, and, in spite of having David sitting beside her, she felt the coil of apprehension tighten in her stomach.

"Is it a long drive to Ko'vik?" Kent asked from the back seat.

"About thirty minutes," Tracy said, wrapping her fingers around each other. Not long enough to relax, and too long to be feeling like this.

She untwisted her fingers, and smoothed the denim of her skirt. Was a skirt too dressy for a visit to her mother? What was the protocol for seeing a biological parent who hadn't been a part of your life for three years?

"So what's Kolvik like?" David asked, his quiet question pulling her out of a most uncomfortable place.

"A lot like Preston. Small. Community-oriented. Not a lot of industry."

"It was a government job that got Jack to move from Grande Prairie to Kolvik. I was always surprised that Emily agreed to it."

"It's a nice town to raise kids in. They have three don't they?"

David smiled. "Yeah. They're great kids. A great family. Lots of fun. My brother and I spent much of our childhood at the Verheeg's place."

"Hence your relationship with Heather." Tracy injected a light tone into her voice. The woman was dead. She didn't need to be jealous of her.

"The original high-school sweetheart. Except I think it was more habit that got us dating than anything else." David sent her an inquisitive look. "And what about you? I know you've got a few old boyfriends."

Tracy laughed lightly. "Just one. Art."

"Oh, yeah. I heard about him."

"How?"

David glanced at her quickly, then turned his attention back to the road, his mouth quirked in a half grin. "I asked around. Dr. Harvey gave me some information. Danielle a little. Some old friends a little more."

"Behind my back? Why didn't you ask me?"

"And you would have told me?"

A flush of embarrassment crept up her neck. "I might have."

"Tracy, Tracy. I see a dog!" Kent called out, breaking the moment.

Tracy turned to where he was pointing. "That's a coyote, honey."

"Anyway, he's not around either," David continued, "so he's either an idiot or you saw the error of your ways and dumped him because you knew you could do better."

Tracy laughed at his comment. Because it was funny. And because it made her feel good and cared for. "Maybe a bit of both," she said with a light flirtatious tone to her voice.

"Maybe." He flashed her a quick smile. "So how are plans coming on the acreage? Any new developments?"

"Nothing yet. Though I did price out some manufactured homes. They looked pretty good."

And the conversation moved easily to more navigable ground as David and Tracy tested the new boundaries of this place they had come to, and Kent broke in occasionally to point out scenery.

Ten minutes later the Welcome to Kolvik sign flashed past. It would be minutes now.

Tracy pulled a lipstick out of her purse and pulling the visor down to look in the mirror, applied it, disappointed to see that her hand was shaking.

She didn't know why she was primping. Self-protection or a deep-seated desire to show her mother that she was a capable woman? The desire every daughter has to have her mother's approval, spoken or unspoken?

"You look good, Tracy," David said. *His* approval warmed her heart.

"Thanks. I just feel I should look my best."

"Where are we?" Kent asked, leaning as far as his seatbelt allowed.

"Kolvik," David said. "And I think this is where we need to be." David turned onto a tree-lined street, scattering yellow leaves as he drove. He drove slowly as Tracy counted down the numbers on the houses, her heartbeat growing heavier.

As they got closer, and the houses and yards grew more shabby, Tracy wished once again that she'd been more firm and that David had been less gentlemanly.

Finally David pulled up in front of a small, dingy home. Tracy checked the number scribbled on a piece of paper, stalling for time, putting off what she had been dreading for the past couple of weeks.

David put the truck in gear, resting one arm on the steering wheel, the other on the back of the seat. "Do you want me to come with you?"

Tracy threw him a grateful glance, but shook her head. "No. I need to do this on my own."

"Call me on my cell phone when you're done. I'll come and pick you up."

Tracy just nodded, biting her lip. *Okay, Lord,* she prayed. *You brought me here. I need You to help me out.*

David moved closer to her, slipped his arm over her shoulder and brushed his lips over her temple in a gentle kiss. "I'll be praying for you," he whispered, his breath warm, alive, against her head.

"Thanks." The single word was a faint sound. She turned back to Kent and gave him a quick wave. Then she drew in a long, slow breath, pulled open the door and stepped out. She paused at the cracked sidewalk leading to the house, glancing back at David's truck, wishing he would leave. He must have gotten the hint because she saw him put it in gear and then he slowly pulled away, waving at her with his free hand, Kent looking out the back window.

So. Future hope moved away to deal with past hurts. She had to keep the two separate from each other if she was going to make it through this visit.

Another long, slow breath, wishing her heart wasn't pushing up against her throat. She walked up to the door. Hesitated. So much easier just to turn around and walk away. To keep her mother in the past, to keep her apart from Tracy's current existence.

But Tracy knew it wasn't that easy. She would always wonder if maybe this time things would be different. The What if that she had clung to again and again as a child was not so easily extinguished. Even though she had been shown different time and time again, a small corner of Tracy's heart nurtured a picture-book fantasy of a loving relationship with her mother.

It was that fantasy that made Tracy curl her fingers into a fist and knock on the door. Lightly first, then a little louder.

There. It was done and there was no turning back.

She waited, each second slipping past like molasses.

Her mother wasn't home.

Wait. Just wait.

Then a muffled noise from inside the house. A dull thud. Then the sound of a chair scraping across the floor. Tracy pulled in another long, steadying breath, and unconsciously fingered her hair back from her face, rubbed her lips together to smooth out her lipstick.

The door opened.

And Velma stood blinking in the light, her graying hair a tangle of curls, mascara smudged under her eyes, her face pale in the afternoon sun.

And drunk as a pirate.

Chapter Ten

Emily's parents were here already. He recognized Linda and Stanley's car parked beside Jack and Emily's. David ran his fingers through his hair, checked it in the mirror and flipped the visor up. He was almost as nervous as he knew Tracy was. Only his nervousness was an interconnected web of guilt woven of his feelings for Tracy and the heavy meaning of this day.

"Is this where we are going?" Kent asked, setting his book aside. "This is a nice house. I like this house. Are the people nice?"

"Yes, they are. The nicest you'll ever meet." David drew in a deep breath as he helped Kent out of the truck. *Help me through this, Lord,* he prayed. *Give me the right words, the right actions. Help me be kind and fair. And honest. That would be the hardest part.*

Together they walked to the door and knocked.

Seconds later the door was yanked open. "David,

you're finally here," Emily cried out, raising her arms to hug him. Then she stopped as her gaze fell on Kent.

David rested his hand lightly on the little boy's head, wondering what thoughts and fears were slipping through his mind. "Emily, I'd like you to meet Kent Cordell. He's a friend of mine who I invited along for a visit."

Emily's frown showed her confusion. "Today?"

David heard a myriad of emotions behind her terse question. Again he felt a familiar pinch of guilt over the fact that his feelings about today didn't mesh with hers or the rest of the family's. Good thing they weren't going to meet Tracy.

"He's a good friend." David caught Emily's eye and telegraphed a warning. "His mom isn't home and I asked him to come along."

Emily thankfully caught the hint. "Well, then, Kent, come on in." She stood aside but as David passed her she stroked his arm. "I've been praying for you," she said softly. "Today is going to be a hard day for you."

Not in the way Emily was thinking. He gave her a careful smile and followed her into the house.

"The family is in the living room," Emily said. "Harmony and Rachel are downstairs playing with makeup. Max is watching them. I'll take Kent there."

David caught a glimpse of Emily's parents with Emily's younger brother and sister sitting in the living room, paging through a photo album. The heaviness of the atmosphere seeped into the kitchen. He squared his shoulders, relinquished Kent to Emily's care and stepped into the living room and his past.

Linda Verheeg got slowly to her feet, her face crumpling as she saw David. "How are you doing, my boy?" She sniffed as she slipped her arms around him. David awkwardly returned her hug, wishing he could absorb Linda's pain as Heather's mother started crying in his arms. "I'm sorry," she said, as she drew away, her voice twisting downward. "This day is even harder than I thought it would be." She wiped her cheeks with the heel of her hand, smiling tremulously up at him. "I can't imagine what it's like for you."

David was glad she couldn't. Linda would be disappointed. On the first anniversary of Heather's death he couldn't even generate more than a nostalgic smudge of sorrow. Though he wondered if he should have come, he knew he owed this family too much to stay away. Coming to the anniversary of a beloved daughter's death was the least he could do.

"David. Good to see you. How's your work?"

David turned with relief to Stanley, Heather's father and a more stable topic of conversation. "It's great, really good," he said, edging away from Linda who was now being held by Emily who had returned from downstairs. "I'm enjoying the challenge of the business."

"Come. Sit down." Stanley indicated an empty chair and love seat and David lowered himself into the latter. "Jack and I were wondering when you were going to come. I'm glad you did." Stanley angled his chin in his wife's direction. "Linda wasn't looking forward to this day and didn't want to be in Grande Prairie. Having you here makes it more meaningful."

David just nodded, unsure of what to say. He was

never good at the soothing stuff. Even during Heather's funeral he had found that it was easier if he said nothing rather than the wrong thing.

"So, are you making your mark in the community?" Jack asked, turning the conversation to more practical matters. "Emily said you had a bit of a tough go at first."

"Hard to walk in the footsteps of Dr. Harvey, but I'm managing to build trust," he said, leaning back into the chair, thankful to be discussing something he could navigate less awkwardly. "He's got a good clinic and a great staff."

Tracy slipped through his mind and he almost blushed. What would they think of him if they knew that he already had a girlfriend? Or whatever one called a few dates with Tracy. A few stolen kisses.

"It takes time to work into an established practice, but I'm sure you can do it, David. You are a very capable man of many talents." Stanley opened the top button of his suit jacket, leaned back in his chair and smiled a fatherly smile. "I had such high hopes for you and Heather."

David shifted in his chair, his mind scrambling for something to say that didn't sound insincere when he felt a light hand on his shoulder. Linda stood beside him, her features wavering. "David, we have a gift for you."

She drew him away from Jack and Stanley and took him to the empty space on the love seat. As he sat down she handed him a large square parcel.

"Emily and Sandra made it just for you."

He gave Emily and her younger sister a quick smile.

Sandra moved to the floor at his feet. Out of the corner of his eye David saw Michael, Emily's youngest brother angle David a quick smile and leaned forward, watching.

David slowly pulled the paper off the package, sensing the family's expectations hovering around him. He lifted the lid of the box and pulled out a photograph album in Heather's favorite candy-apple-red.

"It's beautiful," David said softly, touching the cover lightly, feeling like a fraud.

Linda reached over and opened the album to the first page.

"This is our favorite picture of the two of you," Linda was saying, touching the page as if trying to bring the picture to life.

David glanced down.

And was surprised at the pain that clenched his heart at the picture of Heather, vitally alive, laughing at the camera from the security of David's arms. The camera had caught her in mid-laugh, her head coyly tipped to one side, the sun haloing her long blond hair flowing away from her face. The hair that she had lost bit by bit as chemicals fought their battle inside her body, pulverizing the good with the bad. He looked more serious than she did, his dark eyes slightly narrowed, his mouth in a half smile.

Nostalgia slipped over him. Heather had been a beautiful woman, a good friend, a sister, a beloved daughter. The loss of that was something he could sincerely mourn on this day.

Tracy's head hurt. Her eyelids felt too small and too dry and a jangling pressure built behind her eyes.

Why did she expect any different from her mother? Why had she believed things could change?

It was David's quiet expectation that had brought her to this place. His unspoken disappointment in her seeming lack of forgiveness. She had tried to win his approval and had paid for it with her tears.

She wiped the tears from her eyes as she walked aimlessly down the street. Each thudding heartbeat sent a new wave of hurt coursing through her body, hurt that felt like a betrayal of her pride and her own common sense.

How could she have been so naive? So stupid?

All these years and she still hadn't learned?

She pulled a tissue out of her purse, blew her nose and wiped her eyes, angry that her mother could still pull out such strong emotions. Seeing her mother drunk was nothing new, she reminded herself, stuffing the damp tissue in her pocket. The rank, dull smell of alcohol was as much a part of her life with her mother as the scent of baking bread had been associated with Danielle's mom.

It was the death of a momentary hope that she was grieving. That was all.

She stopped a moment, marshaling her defenses, drawing on anger to erase the weakness of her tears. Her mother wasn't worth them.

Lord, You are the only one who is faithful. The only one.

She repeated the prayer a couple of times, making it a part of the moment. She wanted Danielle.

She wanted David.

She thought of his concern, his kiss. More than anything she wanted to be with him. To have him hold her in his arms and tell her it was okay. He still cared for her.

But he wasn't expecting her. The only option open to her was wandering around Kolvik and phoning David after a suitable interval.

And tell him what? Oh, I had a lovely visit with my mom. I ate. She drank.

Better to do what she usually did when friends asked about Velma.

Lie and smile. In spite of his expectations, or maybe because of them, David didn't need to know the reality of her life. Not yet.

She didn't even look back as she strode the rest of the way down the street toward a corner store. The owner wouldn't let her use the phone, but he would let her use the phone book to look up Emily and Jack's address.

Ten minutes later she stood in front of the kind of house she used to dream of as a child. One and a half stories, gabled dormers, mullioned bay windows. Neatly clipped shrubs cozying up to the house. Trees sheltering it on either side. Even with half of the leaves off the trees the scene was still catalog-perfect.

Tracy ran her hands up and down the strap of her purse. Maybe she'd been hasty in making her plans. Through the bay window she saw David's broad shoulders, his careless hair. Tracy recognized Emily standing beside him, her hand on his shoulder. An unfamiliar woman sat beside him on the couch pointing at something on his lap. They looked cozy. Complete.

She was about to turn around when the side door burst open and a group of kids came flying out the side door, yelling and laughing.

One of them was Kent. He was chasing a squealing

young girl, her arms cupped around her head as he squirted her with a water pistol.

Kent lifted his pistol and was about to drench the girl again, when he caught sight of Tracy. A huge smile split his face. "Tracy, Tracy. You came," he called out, running toward her, reaching out his arms as if he hadn't seen her for months instead of minutes.

Pure, sweet love laced her heart as she crouched down to catch him. Hold him close as a mother would.

Kent gave her a quick hug, then pulled back, waving his green plastic pistol at the three children who still raced around, laughing and spraying. "Those are my friends."

One of the girls had stolen the other boy's water pistol and was chasing him. He ran over to Tracy and ducked behind her, taunting the girls from the safety of politeness.

As the girl looked at Tracy, she lowered her weapon and narrowed her eyes, as if trying to place Tracy herself.

"I know you," the girl said. "I saw you at church. You sat with us."

Tracy nodded as she pushed herself to her feet. "And you're Rachel." Though this Rachel had black-rimmed eyes and bright-red lipstick smeared unevenly over her mouth.

"Do you want to come inside?" Rachel asked, gesturing with her pistol toward the house. "Uncle David is here too."

"Come on," Kent said, tugging on her hand. "They have munchies. You can have some too."

Tracy hesitated, while Kent kept up the gentle pressure on her hand. Then through the window she saw David lift his head and her heart fluttered as she caught his eye. The sudden yearning she felt for him, for the need to attach herself to the good part of her life swarmed over her.

She followed Kent and the other children into the house.

"Mom, we got company," Rachel called out, kicking her running shoes off in the porch. She turned to Tracy. "C'mon. You can keep your shoes on."

Emily met them in the kitchen, a faint frown marring her forehead as she looked from Rachel to Tracy.

"May I help you?" she asked, the polite but cool tone of her voice barring Tracy's entrance into the cozy family setting Tracy saw just beyond her.

"She's a friend of Uncle David," Rachel explained. "Kent says she came with them." Rachel sauntered into the living room and dropped on the arm of the love seat David sat in. "Your friend Tracy is here," she said nonchalantly.

"My goodness, girl, what have you done to your face?" the woman beside David asked in a shocked tone. "You look like a clown. And you're soaking wet. Go wash your face." Linda got up at the same time as David did, glancing at Tracy with a frown very similar to Emily's.

Tracy's heart dipped. And when David came into the kitchen, holding a large book, his shoulders hunched, a vague smile on his face, she knew she should have gone with plan C. Stay away and wait.

"Hey, Tracy. What are you doing here?"

If it wasn't for the fact that they had such an interested audience, she would have turned tail and left. Of course it was probably because of that interested audience that David seemed so withdrawn.

"I came here…well…my mom wasn't home."

David's careful smile faded into a puzzled frown. "I thought she was expecting you?"

"I thought so too." She had started this story in front of so great a cloud of witnesses, she had to carry it through. "So, instead of wandering around Kolvik, I thought I'd come and see where you and Kent were. Then he came outside and it seemed kind of silly just to keep walking." Which was the truth, in fact but not in intent.

"Of course. Sure." David made a vague gesture in the direction of the living room. "Come. Sit down. Do you want some coffee? Or tea?"

"I'm okay." Tracy kept her eyes on him, trying to read this changed attitude. In the truck he had been all encouragement and solicitation.

Now he acted as if he didn't want her here.

She could leave, but Kent still stood beside her, still clinging to her hand. So she decided to brazen it out.

She greeted Emily, who hadn't moved. Tracy glanced quickly around the full living room, spotting an empty chair beside a young boy who gave her a polite smile and returned to the book he was reading. She moved to it and sat, and Kent sat on the floor at her feet.

"Rachel, you're soaked. You go change and then you can start a movie for you and Harmony and the boys," Emily said, nudging her daughter, who still lounged on the armrest of the love seat, oblivious to her grand-mother's instructions. "There's a rented one on top of the television in the family room downstairs." Emily glanced back. "Max. Harmony. Take Kent downstairs to watch a movie."

Kent looked up at Tracy as if seeking permission, which she reluctantly granted.

Once Kent left, Tracy would be on the edge of this family gathering. Besides, she felt a heaviness in the room that put her on edge, made her feel even more of an intruder.

"Linda, Stanley, I'd like you to meet Tracy. I drove her here to visit her mother. Tracy, these are Emily's parents. Jack and Emily you already know. This is Sandra, Emily's sister, and the scholar beside you is Michael."

The older woman on the love seat gave Tracy a terse nod, Stanley reached over and shook her hand. Sandra didn't look at her and Michael gave her another quick smile.

"Nice to meet you, Tracy," Linda said with a cool smile. "Are you Kent's mother?"

"No. I…uh…work with David," she said, carefully feeling her way around the conversation and her relation-ship with David. "Kent has been staying at my place."

Emily looked puzzled and glanced at David. "I thought you said he didn't have a place."

David glanced over his shoulder, as if to make sure that Kent was out of earshot. "He's staying with Tracy because his mother is gone and we don't know where she is. Kent's been hanging around the clinic. A couple of times he ended up staying in there overnight." David glanced over at Tracy, his expression unreadable.

And Tracy felt a finger of apprehension snake down her back at his comments, so distant and removed.

"That is so sad. Have you called social services?" Linda, the woman on the love seat, was asking.

"Tracy has a friend who works for the department," David said.

"If there's anything Emily and I can do to help, David, let us know," Jack said with a light frown.

Tracy wanted to jump up and shout out, "I'm the one who found him. I'm the one who's going to help him. You don't even know him." But she checked her sudden anger.

David was fidgeting, rubbing one thumb over the other, tapping his foot lightly on the carpet. His body language fairly screamed uncomfortable.

She shouldn't have come.

"You didn't get a chance to finish looking at Heather's album," Linda said, laying the bright red book on David's lap.

Heather. The dead girlfriend. And from where she was sitting Tracy could see the large picture on the first page. No surprises there. She was beautiful and she was blond. It seemed Tracy was cursed to be surrounded by a bevy of blond clones. What did surprise Tracy were the different kinds of jealousy that grabbed her like unwelcome old friends.

There was jealousy of the woman who had at one time held David's heart. But layered through that was jealousy over how this family clearly missed their daughter.

"Emily put this together shortly after Heather's funeral," the older lady was saying. She turned to Tracy. "Our daughter, Heather, was engaged to David. She died today, exactly one year ago." Tracy reeled in surprise. Heather had been David's fiancée.

Chapter Eleven

Tracy felt an icy hand of pain drag at her as she tried to force her now-stiff lips to smile. David was looking intently at her, but she let her gaze skitter away.

A fiancée was much more than a girlfriend, a relationship David had spoken casually of. Why had David lied to her? What had he been trying to hide?

But in spite of the cold jealousy that pulled on her she heard the hitch in Linda's voice. "I'm sorry to hear that," she murmured politely as she got up.

This was getting more awkward by the minute. "I'm sorry, I should go."

"No, no, sit down," Linda said, getting up from her place beside David. "Would you like to see the album as well?"

It was the last thing she wanted to do, but she had crashed this party, she might as well see this through. So she got up and obediently sat beside David, careful not to sit too close. Linda sat beside her on the arm of the love seat.

David's reticence was like a wall between them, clear but impenetrable. It shouldn't matter what his relationship with Heather had been. It shouldn't matter to her that he had at one time contemplated marrying this stunningly beautiful woman.

But it did.

"This was Heather at the Faith Alive womens' retreat," Emily was saying, reaching past David to turn the page. Another picture of Heather smiling surrounded by a group of women. This wasn't going to be easy. "She loved going to them. Have you ever been, Tracy?"

Tracy shook her head. Another mark against her.

"It's a wonderful opportunity to renew your faith. Heather was such a strong Christian." Emily turned another page. "Oh, and here's a really nice series of Heather when she was at camp. From our church. And of course, here's David."

Tracy forced herself to look down at a picture of Heather and David, their arms around each other. David was looking at the camera, Heather at him, her heart in her eyes, clearly in love with the man who also made Tracy's heart flutter.

He had asked this woman to marry him. To be his life's partner.

Why are you so upset about this? she asked herself. Saying "I care about you" and giving a few kisses doesn't give you ownership.

She suffered through photos of Heather doing more wonderful things with David, her family, her friends, each picture adding one more ache, one more insecurity to Tracy's already bruised emotions.

Heather had been loved by her family. Heather had been loved by David. The first Tracy had never truly experienced. The latter she had received a taste of and wanted more.

But how could she compare to Heather? A girl who went to Christian retreats. Who loved and was loved by her family. Could she stand to be, once again, second-best?

She wanted to leave but was held here by the gentle snare of politeness and, in spite of herself and the solid proof of his previous love, by David's presence.

And that was the worst of it.

"This was toward the end," Linda said, gently turning a page, smoothing her hand over it. Heather sat up in a hospital bed, her smile forced, a brightly colored turban covering her head. Not a strand of blond hair in sight. David sat beside her, his arm around her shoulders, looking at her with a mixture of sorrow and love.

Tracy swallowed. Even with all her hair gone, tubes snaking out of her arms, Heather still looked angelic. Beautiful. A courageous woman with the man who loved her at her side.

"David spent a lot of time with her at the end," Linda said softly. "He quit work to take care of her. He was very devoted."

It was as if each word she spoke pushed David higher and higher up a pedestal, closer to Heather and farther away from her. David, the paragon of virtue and devoted fiancé.

Then, at last, Linda closed the book, giving it to David. He ran his hands lightly over the cover.

"Thanks for this," he said to Emily, placing the book carefully on the low coffee table. "It's something I'll treasure for a long time."

Emily reached over and hugged him. "I'm so glad you live close by, David. It means so much to me."

Tracy fought self-pity and the most unwelcome urge to cry. Today had been bad enough without having to watch the members of this family laying their claim to a man she was falling in love with. A man she didn't have anything to offer that matched what this family was to him.

She had to leave.

"Excuse me," she said softly, getting up, making it seem as if she simply needed to go to the washroom.

She picked up her purse and left the room. She went downstairs, following the sounds of laughter to a large, open room. Four faces were turned with rapt expressions to the television.

Kent barely noticed her when she came and crouched down beside him. "I'm going to go for a walk. When Dr. David is finished visiting, tell him I'll meet you guys at the Rotary Park, okay?"

Kent nodded, his attention on the television.

Tracy left quietly, feeling like a sneak as she closed the door behind her. She should have gone upstairs again and apologized for leaving but she was afraid if she did she would start to cry. And she had done enough of that in her life. She walked quickly down the driveway, staying out of sight of the front-room windows, and then struck out toward the park, a few blocks away.

She'd had better days, she thought, as she strode down the walk. Much better days.

But then, she'd had worse as well.

Only God is faithful, she reminded herself. Only God is faithful.

She was sitting on a bench, her arms crossed over her stomach, watching a group of kids throwing sand at each other. David parked his truck, keeping his eyes on Tracy as if afraid she would run away again.

Once he'd found out from Kent that she'd left the party, he had stayed as long as he deemed polite, then he'd left. Guilt over his deception with Tracy battled his obligation to Heather's family. But his future won over his past and as soon as he dared, he left, resisting the family's gentle pressure.

"Can you stay here, please?" He turned to Kent who was sitting in the front seat.

Kent just nodded and turned his attention back to a battery-powered handheld game Max, Emily's son, had given him.

Tracy looked up when he approached, then looked away. At least she didn't run away. He sat down beside her, resting his elbows on his knees, rooting around for the right words, the correct thing to say to her.

"I'm sorry about the family thing," he said softly, wanting to touch her. To reconnect with her life and vitality. "I should have told you why we were getting together."

"That's okay," she interrupted, her voice soft. Reasonable and unemotional. "It was none of my business."

But David wished she would make it some of her

business. Wished she would open up to him a bit more so he could reassure her that Heather was in the past. That their engagement hadn't been as real as the family had alluded to. That Heather had made it up and he had played along with it because what did it matter? She was dying and it was such a small thing to give to her.

But he didn't even know if it mattered to Tracy. If he mattered to her.

She got up. "I shouldn't have barged in like that. I'm sorry." Her polite smile kept his confidences buttoned away.

As David followed her to the truck he bit back a sigh of frustration. It was as if the kiss between them before he'd dropped her off had never happened. As if he had imagined that precious moment of vulnerability she had shown just before she left the truck.

"Look what I got, Tracy," Kent said, waving the handheld game at her as she got in the truck. "Max gave it to me. He's a nice guy."

"Wow. You'll have to show me how it works," Tracy said, slipping her arm protectively around the boy and pulling him close.

"So you had no idea your mother wasn't going to be home?" David asked, grabbing for anything that would start some type of conversation.

Tracy's only reply was a quick shake of her head. "Can I try?" Tracy asked Kent, reaching for the game.

They bent over the tiny screen, electronic blips signaling Tracy's progress or lack of it. Tracy was completely relaxed around Kent. Smiling and laughing.

But all the way home, she not only avoided looking

at David and giving him any indication of what was going on in her mind, she said nothing at all.

He pulled up in front of her apartment, slowing more than necessary, trying to buy some time. Tracy slipped her purse over her shoulder and unbuckled Kent, fussing over him.

When he came to a stop, she already had one hand on the door. How could he stop her? He didn't know if she even cared that Heather had at one time been his fiancée instead of the girlfriend he'd said she was.

He didn't know because she didn't ask.

"Thanks for the ride," she said, favoring him with a quick glance as she started to open the door.

"Wait a minute." He took a chance and touched her shoulder. "I, uh…"

Quick. Talk.

"I feel like I should explain…about Heather."

"David, I told you, it's none of my business."

"I'd like it to be," he said softly, not letting go of her even as she tried to ease away. "I'm sorry I didn't tell you about Heather. It just…didn't seem important enough to bring up."

She still wouldn't look at him. Still wouldn't meet his gaze.

"It's okay, David. I understand."

Empty words. Blanks meant to carefully push him away even as she pulled from his touch.

"Do you have everything, Kent?" she asked the little boy, taking his hand. "We should go."

Kent nodded and turned to David, favoring him with a quick smile. "Bye, Dr. David. See you later."

He scrambled out of the truck after Tracy who strode up the walk without a second glance.

As the apartment door fell shut behind them, David slammed his hand on the steering wheel in frustration.

Tracy knew exactly how to freeze him out. It was like trying to grab hold of a mist, trying to talk to a wavering reflection in water. Always changing, never the same.

Complicated. Way too complicated.

He pushed the truck in gear and spun away from the curb, taking small satisfaction in the squeal of the tires and the revving of the engine.

"So. How did it go?"

Danielle's overly cheery voice grated, but Tracy dismissed her own reaction. Petty. Small.

"It didn't," she said, glancing at Kent who lay on the carpet in front of the television, his chin resting in his hands, elbows on the carpet. His bare feet swayed back and forth in time to the lively music of the video. He would be okay for a while.

"And why not?" Danielle sounded slightly more subdued, and Tracy felt a little more gracious. "She wasn't home?"

"She wasn't sober." The sight of her mother all dressed up and wavering in the doorway of her home kept creeping like a snake into her mind, seeping like poison into every part of her life that Tracy thought she had salvaged.

Danielle's silence spoke of shared memories and sorrows, and Tracy had to bite her lip against the newly resurrected pain. Why did her mother manage to do this again and again?

"So I left and ended up at Emily's, where David was, and found out that dear Heather, the girlfriend, wasn't just a girlfriend. She was his fiancée."

"They were engaged?"

"And the reason David had to make a trip to Kolvik was to commemorate the first anniversary of Heather's death with her family." She slid down to the floor, still watching Kent, her hand wrapped around the phone. She and Danielle had spent many an hour this way, sharing, talking, even after seeing each other all day at school.

"That's not very long."

"And she was not only the girl he wanted to marry, she was a wonderful, kind, caring Christian woman who has two normal parents, who loved animals, wanted children and desired world peace." Tracy bit her lip. "As opposed to materialistic and shallow me who's never been to a Faith Alive women's retreat, scarlet woman that I am, and whose heart beats faster at the idea of ten acres, a milk cow and twelve chickens."

"Lost the clothes line?"

"Upgraded to clothes dryer." Tracy sighed. "They were going to get married, Danielle. I bet he's just going out with me 'cause he's lonely. I mean, look how long it took me to get over Art. And *he* was a jerk." Tracy found a loose string on the bottom cuff of her blue jeans and tugged on it.

"Which I take it Heather was not."

"She was beautiful and kind and caring. Which makes me wonder why David got involved with me."

"Guys don't like to be alone much. Mom was only dead six months and Dad was already dating."

"Sounds like you still have issues with Dad over that."

Danielle sighed heavily. "I do. But the boys didn't seem to have huge problems with it at all. Typical guys."

"Well, at least your dad didn't get remarried. That would have been harder."

"Why should he get remarried when he's got me?" Tracy heard the edge in Danielle's words.

"You need to find someone of your own."

"I think Anthony might be it. He's caring and sensitive and that means a lot after living with my brothers so long."

"A good man is hard to find."

"And you don't think you have?"

Tracy pursed her lips, as if considering. "David's not perfect, but…" Tracy tugged on another string, fraying the cuff even further. "I can't get past this engaged thing. Heather died only a year ago. Maybe I'm just rebound. Like you said, guys don't like to be alone." Tracy sighed out her frustration and sorrow.

"Okay, I hear a lot of soul-searching in that exhalation of breath."

"And that infamous *L*-word. As in falling in love." Tracy sighed again, hesitant to speak, yet, in true girl-fashion, wanting to share the emotions. To make them more real by saying them aloud.

"Oh boy."

"Oh man, more like. And just as that's happening I discover he's got this perfect, blond, strong Christian fiancée who died fighting a courageous battle. She sounded like she could be a lot of fun and she was pretty."

"Ghosts are tough competition. They're frozen in

time and all that's left are memories that can't be tarnished or changed. And you know how that works."

"Yeah. You only remember the good things. That's how my mother got to me all the time."

"Aw, Trace. I'm so sorry."

"It's okay." The music slipped away and Tracy craned her neck to see what Kent was up to. The movie had changed pace and he was still watching.

"Trouble is, I'm phoning for another reason," Danielle said softly. "I got a call on my cell phone Saturday evening. Edgar Stinson."

"What did he want?"

"He claims to be Kent's grandfather."

Dread caught Tracy in an icy grip. "No way. He can't be. Kent always called Steve uncle."

"It doesn't matter right now anyway. We still haven't found Kent's mom, and she has first say in what happens to the boy. Don't worry."

"And what if you don't find her? Do I start worrying then?"

"I'll do the worrying. You just make sure Kent is safe."

"So far so good." Tracy pushed herself up to her feet. "Hey, it's been a long day. I gotta go."

"Okay. Hey, girl, I'm sorry. I shouldn't have pushed you."

"Don't worry. You know the song. Fool me once, shame on you. Fool me twice…"

"Or four or five."

More like two hundred and five. "Don't worry. Just a reminder of why I try not to think of her too much. Gotta go. Take care."

Tracy hung up the phone and pulled her hands over her face. Too much information to carry for one day. Edgar claiming to be Kent's grandfather. Her mother. Heather.

David.

She focused on what she had to do for now. Keep Kent safe. That was all she needed to do. She went into the living room and dropped onto the floor beside Kent. He looked up at her with a light frown. "When can we go see my kitty?"

Tracy felt a light hitch to her heart. "Dr. David has it now. You'll have to ask him."

Kent just nodded and turned back to the television. Tracy sat beside him, staring unseeingly at the television, her mind a kaleidoscope of thoughts, pictures. Impressions.

The credits came up and Tracy turned off the television. "Bedtime, little guy," she said.

"But I don't want to go to bed," he said, a faint whine entering his voice. "I'm not tired." But his red ears and rosy cheeks told her another story.

"I won't leave you alone," she said softly, gently stroking his still-bath-damp hair away from his face. "I'll stay with you until you fall asleep. Okay?" Last night, she'd let Kent fall asleep in her bed and then she'd moved him onto the foam mattress she had laid out on the floor.

Kent sighed lightly, then nodded.

She supervised his toothbrushing, made sure he went to the bathroom, rationed out his last drink of the night and ushered him into her bedroom. When he was settled in her bed, she lay down on the covers beside him.

The light of her bedside table made his dark eyes look like twin pools of night and cast gentle shadows over his soft features. She felt safe and snug in here with him. Tucked away from all the concerns that crouched outside the door, waiting for her insecure self to come out so they could dig their tenacious claws into her. All the voices that had echoed through her life: unworthy, unimportant, unnecessary.

"Do you want to learn a bedtime prayer?" Tracy asked, leaning on her elbow, dragging out the moment.

Kent frowned. "What's a prayer?"

Good question. "It's talking to God." Or begging Him for help. Tracy couldn't stop a faint flush of guilt. She knew she didn't pray as sincerely or as often as she should. Heather'd probably never had to worry about foxhole prayers. Heather's life was probably one long prayer.

Those thoughts were for outside the bedroom. She was in here with Kent, and he was her focus for now.

"How will He hear me?" Kent asked, running his fingers over the sheet Tracy had tucked over his chest. "I thought He was in heaven."

"He's everywhere." Tracy covered his hand with hers and squeezed lightly, a feeling of maternal love blossoming in her. "And even better, He never sleeps."

"Ever?" Kent pulled his head back, his frown deepening the dark of his eyes. "Not even when He's tired?"

Tracy smiled and toyed with his fingers. "He never gets tired and He never even yawns." At the mention of the word Tracy stifled her own yawn.

"Okay. Teach me the prayer."

"Actually it's more of a song. It's called 'Jesus, Tender Shepherd, Hear Me' and it was written a long time ago."

"I don't sing good," Kent whispered.

"That's okay," Tracy whispered back. "Neither do I. But no one else can hear us except God, and He thinks we sound great." She took a gentle breath and began:

Jesus, tender shepherd, hear me,
Bless this little lamb tonight,
Through the darkness be thou near me,
Keep me safe till morning light.

Kent blinked, then smiled sleepily. "Sing it again."

And as she did, her mind slipped back to other nights when her mother had lain on the bed with her, just as she was doing with Kent now. Her mother's voice surrounding her, comforting her. Her hand lying gently on her arm, protecting her and keeping her safe. Only it had happened so seldom.

"Is Jesus tender shepherd watching over my mommy too?" Kent whispered, his voice wavering.

Tracy gently stroked his hair back from his forehead. "Yes, He is," she said quietly. Her own feelings for Kent wove through her memories of her mother, of evenings spent together. Of the love she had seen glimpses of.

Please, Lord, do watch over Kent's mom. Wherever she is. In spite of her own affection for him, she also knew how Kent felt. The yearning he had for his own mother. And again she felt the twinge of jealousy. And behind it, anger.

Children are such a gift. Did her mother not see that? Did Kent's mother not see that?

She kissed Kent again and with her thumbs, stroked away the tears that had slipped out of the corners of his eyes. "You have a good sleep, Kent," she said.

He just nodded, turned his head and closed his eyes.

Tracy stayed with him until his breathing deepened and slowed and his fingers began twitching.

She carefully eased herself off the bed and out of the room, leaving the door open slightly so she could hear him if he cried out.

The apartment was suddenly horribly quiet. And empty. She shuddered and walked over to her stereo, turning it on. Light classical music drifted out of the speakers and she turned it up just a little. Enough to push away the silence.

Shattered by the buzzing of the intercom.

Her heart lurched at the unexpected sound and she ran for it, hoping its shrill sound wouldn't wake Kent.

"Hello?" she said, wondering who would come calling this time of the night.

"Hi, Tracy. It's David. I know it's late, but can I come up?"

Tracy pressed her hand against her chest, stilling a heartbeat that, if anything, had increased even more. What did David want from her? Hadn't the day been enough of an emotional drain? Did she really want to talk to him when they couldn't find anything to say on the long drive home?

But the thought of David standing on her doorstep altered the rhythm of her heart, tugged at deeper, slightly thrilling emotions and before she could convince herself this wasn't a good idea, she pressed the button that would unlock the door.

While she waited, she smoothed her hands over her hair, straightened her shirt.

A quick knock at her apartment door made her swallow, take a deep breath and walk unsteadily to open it.

David stood in the hallway, his shoulders hunched, his hands tucked in the front pockets of his blue jeans. He had changed to a loose, dark sweater that accented the hazel of his eyes as it flowed over the breadth of his shoulders.

"Hey, there," he said, shifting his weight to his other foot as he gave her a careful smile, held her gaze with deep-set eyes. "I didn't know if you'd be up, but I saw your light on." He shrugged. "So I took a chance."

"Come on in." She stood aside, holding the door with two hands for support, her heart fluttering in her throat as he stepped past her.

"Danielle phoned me…" He lifted one shoulder in a vague gesture, as if unsure of what else he really did want to say. "Told me about Edgar. I just wanted to make sure everything was okay with Kent."

Tracy carefully closed the door, as if her very life depended on making sure the latch clicked just so, disappointment mingling with her practical nature. Of course David would want to check on Kent.

She didn't know what to say either, so she fixed on the ordinary. The easy fix and a quick escape. "Did you want some tea or coffee?" she asked, turning and walking past him to the kitchen.

"That's okay. I don't want to be any trouble."

You already are, she thought, wishing her heart wouldn't jump around her chest like some hyperactive child just at the sound of his deep voice.

"I often drink tea at night," she said, pulling out her kettle. Filling it with water. A simple job she performed every day. But usually just for herself. Danielle when she came over. Sometimes for the occasional visitor that she would have.

The last man she had done this for was Art.

Great, she thought, plunking the kettle down on the stove and snapping on the flame underneath it. Why not pull him out of your messy memory chest too? You don't have enough ammunition from today to keep yourself permanently humbled and humiliated?

Enough. Enough.

Cast your cares on the Lord and He will sustain you; He will never let the righteous fall. The words from Psalm 52 slipped into her mind. Like a storm-tossed shipwreck survivor she grabbed and clung to the passage, letting the words settle in. Cast your cares on the Lord.

She imagined herself letting go of the burden of hurt pride and disappointments, letting them float away for Jesus to pick up.

She took a long breath, letting the peace settle deeper.

She didn't throw herself into your arms, so now what are you going to do? Stay here and try to begin the talk you couldn't manage in the truck? Try to explain about Heather and get yourself snarled even further in the tangle of trying to figure out what, if any, relationship you and Tracy had?

David sighed and sank back into the soft embrace of the armchair, immediately regretting his choice. It would be impossible to make a graceful exit out of here if things went really bad.

Guess he was committed now.

When Danielle had phoned him to tell him about Edgar Stinson's angry phone call, the first thing David had thought was that he now had a legitimate reason to stop in and see Tracy.

Now he wasn't so sure it had been such a good idea. He'd known Tracy wasn't going to throw herself at him when he came to the door, but he had hoped for a little more than the tight little smile she gave him.

In the kitchen he heard the faint scrape of cups, the clink of spoons and then the splash of water being poured into a teapot.

"Do you need any help?" he asked, trying to work his way out of the chair and into her good graces.

But gravity and spongy cushions held him in their grip.

Tracy came out of the kitchen holding a tray, a careful smile skirting her lips. That was promising.

"It's okay. I'm all done." She set the tray down then frowned at him as he struggled to get to the edge of the chair, his elbows sinking into the soft arms. "I'm sorry," she said, her smile growing warm as he eased his way forward. "I should have warned you about the hostage chair."

Her grin made David grateful for the acrobatics he had to perform to get himself to the edge of the chair. If it made her happy, he was happy.

"I'd say it's taking no prisoners, but I can't seem to get free." David pushed again and inched himself forward enough to shift his center of balance. One more push was all it would take.

"You want some help?" Tracy held out her hand.

David looked up at her smiling face, then grasped her hand. One tug and he was standing up in front of her. But he didn't let go. Couldn't. She was so close he caught the almond smell of her shampoo. He wanted to touch her. Connect.

"Worrying about you and Kent wasn't the only reason I came by," he said softly, still holding her hand.

She didn't say anything, but neither did she pull his hand out of hers.

"I didn't like the way our day ended." He avoided her gaze as he toyed with her fingers, buying time.

One of her nails was blue, and he remembered a grimace of pain when her finger was caught in a cattle squeeze at Doerksens' farm. She was tough. And independent. And she wasn't going to ask him anything.

"I don't know what you mean." She spoke quietly, but didn't pull her hand out of his.

He snared her gaze now. "I know I said it already, but I'm sorry about this afternoon."

She glanced quickly away. "It's okay, David. I came to a family gathering I had no right to attend. If my mother had been…" Then she tried to pull her hands away. Retreat.

But David wouldn't let go so easily. "I should have told you about me and Heather, but I didn't know if you and me were a we or just a you and me trying to figure out if we could be a we." David paused, as his words registered on his befuddled brain. "And may I try that over again? I sound like one of the three little pigs."

Tracy laughed.

Well, he'd accomplished something. He pushed a little further.

"What I'm trying to say is this whole you-and-me thing is at a funny stage. I want it to go somewhere, but I'm not sure if you do. I should have told you about Heather. And I'm sorry."

"It was a shock," Tracy said softly, looking down at their entwined hands.

"I had wanted to break up with her for some time, but our families were so connected. Neighbors, friends and all that. Then when I finally built up the courage, we found out she had cancer. I couldn't break up with her. Then, when we found out it was inoperable, she asked me if I would please propose to her. She didn't want to die single. So I agreed. I'm not sorry I did it." He paused, praying Tracy understood. "I'm just sorry I didn't tell you. And I didn't because it wasn't a big deal to me. It was a small gift I could give her. Nothing more than that."

Tracy's fingers tightened on his, and when she lifted her face, her smile shone like a light in the gloom that had fallen since this afternoon. "You are a wonderful man, David Braun."

"And you are a wonderful person. And I wish I could have met your mother."

Wrong thing to say. Tracy's smile drifted off her face and she lowered her eyes. Just like the last time he mentioned her mother.

But he wasn't going to let her pull away. Not now.

He took a chance, gently ran his finger down her cheek, tucking a strand of hair behind her ear, his hand drifting down to her shoulder and lingering there. She didn't move, but her fingers tightened on his, the deep brown of her eyes growing darker.

Then he bent his head and touched his lips to hers. To his surprise, she responded, then with a gentle murmur, laid her hands on his chest, then slipped into his embrace.

He held her close, his heart drumming, his breathlessness created by this slight woman in his arms.

A sigh of contentment slipped past his lips, teasing her hair as he brushed a light kiss on her temple. He had loved before, but this was new territory to him.

Tracy was nothing like Heather and his feelings for her were richer, stronger and deeper. *This feels so right,* he thought. *Thank you, Lord. This feels so good.*

He brushed his fingers over her face as if trying to draw a response from her. She slipped her arms around him. Held him close.

"No. You can't do that."

The sharp cry of anguish dragged them apart. Sent the emotions of the moment scattering like startled snowbirds.

"No. No. No." Kent ran at David, his arms flailing. Trying to push him away from Tracy, hitting him. "No. You can't. You stay away."

David caught the child's hands and held them as hard as he dared without hurting him. "It's okay, Kent. It's me. Dr. David."

It was like trying to hold on to a thrashing snake. Kent's foot connected with David's shin, his hand twisted out of David's grip and Kent smacked him hard on his stomach.

"Stop it, Kent." Tracy tried to grab the boy, now twisting in David's grip.

"Don't, Tracy. He'll hurt you." David grunted as Kent managed to land another kick.

"You're a bad man. You're bad." Kent wailed, tugging and writhing in David's grasp.

David managed to get Kent's arms behind his back and held the boy close to him, wishing he could absorb the little boy's pain. The obvious sorrow that heaved in his chest.

Kent squirmed once more, then suddenly wilted against David, all the fight gone out of him, sobs now wracking his body.

David crouched down, holding the little boy close, stroking his head lightly as he tried to soothe him. "It's okay, Kent. I'm not the bad man. You know that."

Tracy knelt beside them, her hand on Kent's back, making slow circles, talking quietly to him as well. She bit her lip as her eyes met David's, silent questions and speculation arching between them. The moment was gone, but the promise of it lay in her wistful smile.

Kent's cries slowly subsided, his tears soaking through David's sweater. David didn't dare let go until he knew for sure the boy was calmer.

"Did you have a bad dream?" David asked, slowly easing Kent away from him. He wanted to read what he could in the little boy's eyes.

Kent scrubbed the tears from his cheeks with the palms of his hands. Wiped his nose with the sleeve of his pajamas, but kept his head down. "I thought…I thought…" He hiccuped, sucked in a wobbly breath. "I thought you was…was…Uncle Steve."

David frowned at Tracy who nodded at him as if she understood what Kent was talking about.

"But you know he isn't, don't you?" Tracy said quietly. She sat down on the floor and drew the little boy into her arms, cradling him on her lap as she rested her chin on his head. "You know that this is Dr. David."

Kent sniffed and nodded as Tracy rocked him. Soothed him. "Dr. David is a good man. He won't hurt you. Ever. Remember how he helped your kitty? He made it all better. Dr. David knows how to make things better." Her voice was pitched low, her cadence comforting.

David sat down beside her, resting his arm on his upraised knee, smiling at Tracy's defense of him, suddenly feeling like a better person than he actually was.

"Does Dr. David still have my kitty?" Kent whispered, his head tucked into Tracy's neck.

"I do, Kent," David said. "Maybe tomorrow, after work, I can take you to see him?"

Kent sniffed and turned his head slightly, catching David's eye. He blinked and David was pleased to see a smile tremble on his lips. "I miss my kitty," he said quietly. Sniffed again. "And I miss my mommy."

"Of course you do." Tracy gently fingered his hair back from his face. "And I'm sure your mommy misses you."

"I don't wanna go to bed," Kent said. "I'm scared."

"You can stay with us until you fall asleep." Tracy brushed a light kiss on his forehead.

David didn't want to resent this lonely child's intrusion. It was just that a few moments ago he'd expected to end the evening talking to Tracy. Getting to know her better. David held Tracy's gaze, wishing he could convey all the things he had hoped to tell her.

Instead he gently reached over and touched her cheek quickly, before Kent noticed. "I'll put a movie on," he said as he pushed himself off the floor.

Tracy gave him a tremulous smile, and he was gratified to see regret on her face.

Explanations would have to wait. They had time, he reminded himself as he shuffled through the DVDs by Tracy's television. Lots of time.

Chapter Twelve

"I found her," Danielle said. "I found Kent's mom."

Tracy's heart jumped as she turned away from her computer. "Where is she?"

"At the University Hospital in Edmonton. She was transferred there from a hospital in Bonnyville. Someone found her in a motel room over the weekend. She was beat up pretty bad. She's still out of it."

"How did you find her?"

"I'd sent out a notice to the emergency wards and finally got something late Monday afternoon. She's in pretty rough shape. She'll be there awhile. So this morning I put in an application for Kent to become a temporary ward."

"If he goes into care, I want to be considered," Tracy said.

Danielle's silence wasn't reassuring.

"I can do this, Dani. I love this kid. I don't want him to go through the trauma of moving. He's settled into my house. We have a relationship."

"Tracy, it's a one-bedroom apartment."

Tracy clutched the phone tighter. "As soon as my place gets subdivided, I can buy it, take ownership, then move a manufactured home onto the place. Then I'd have lots of room." She'd had the financing in place. All it would take was a phone call once the place was subdivided and things could be set in motion. It would take a couple of weeks to deal with Edgar Stinson, but she had the signed agreement for sale. The rest was up to the lawyers.

"You'll have to have a home study done and we can't base it on future plans, Tracy. We have to work with what you have now."

"But if there's such a need…"

"There is. And of course because of your relationship with Kent, you would be our first consideration, Tracy." Danielle sighed lightly. "Are you sure you want to do this? It's quite a commitment."

Pictures of Kent sitting in her living room, playing with his bricks, sitting at the table eating his food with relish, seeing him off to school in the morning—all flashed through her mind like a slow-motion montage.

"Yes. I'm sure. I love that little guy. And I know how to make him happy."

"That I don't doubt. I'm arranging for Kent to visit his mother in the hospital tomorrow. Would you be able to take him?"

"I don't have a car," she said reluctantly. No vehicle would be one more mark against her taking care of Kent.

"I can arrange for a driver. He'd be going after school anyway."

"Does he have to go, Dani? I mean, she's going to look pretty bad."

"You told me yourself that he misses her."

"I know. I know. I just…" Tracy let the sentence fade away. Dani knew well enough what she thought of Kent's mother. "So what do you think about me taking care of him?"

"This is a huge responsibility, Tracy. You might want to talk to David about it."

"David cares about him too."

"Okay. Your call. I gotta go. I'll keep in touch about the driver."

"And the home study."

"Absolutely. You take care, girlfriend."

"Always." Tracy hung up the phone, rested her face in her hands, her elbows on the desk, relief mixing with apprehension.

She felt a brief flash of jealousy at the thought of Kent seeing his mother. She had grown so close to the little boy, she didn't want to share him. And against her better judgment, she had started making plans, seeing future events with the two of them. And David.

"More work for me?"

The light touch of David's hand on her shoulder spun her around, her heart thumping against her ribs.

"David, you scared me."

He hunched down, putting his face on a level with hers, a gentle smile flitting over his mouth. "Sorry. I tried not to."

He touched her hand lightly, the connection sending a faint shiver up her arm.

She returned his smile. Pressed his hand between hers. "You're a good man, David Braun."

He raised his eyebrows. "Because I didn't try to scare you?"

Tracy, taking another chance, reached out and gently smoothed his hair back from his face. "Yeah. That and a few other things."

His expression was a mixture of puzzlement and pleasure. Tracy chose to focus on the pleasure.

"You never cease to surprise me, Tracy Harris."

She never ceased to surprise herself, she thought.

And maybe someday, if things kept going the way they were, she would dare tell him the entire truth about her life.

But not yet. Not quite yet.

The buzzer sounded and David glanced up from the bills he was sorting. Tracy had gone on a call with Dr. Harvey, and Crystal was working in the back.

A tall, slender woman walked gracefully toward the desk, her glossed lips curved in a half smile as she caught David's eye. She wore a navy tailored suit jacket and matching pants, completely at odds with her feather earrings and the tiny diamond glinting from her nose. Coffee-brown hair flowed over her shoulders, and in the overhead lights David caught the glint of gray threading through the waves.

"Good afternoon. I'm looking for Tracy Harris." Her voice was deep, rough-edged. The voice of a chain-smoker, David thought.

"She's out on a call with our other vet." David got up. "Can I help you?"

"Are you Tracy's co-worker?"

"I'm David Braun, part-owner of the clinic."

"Her boss then." The woman's smile grew as she looked around. "I'm not surprised Tracy ended up working here. She always did love animals." She looked back at David and laughed lightly, holding out a well-manicured hand. "I'm sorry. I should introduce myself. I'm Velma Harris. Tracy's mother."

David couldn't help but stare at the woman that Tracy never wanted to talk about. In all his imaginings, this elegantly off-beat woman was not what he'd expected. He took her hand, shook it.

"You look a little surprised," Velma said, scooping her hair back from her face. "I take it Tracy didn't tell you much about me."

Precious little. "Tracy is a private person."

"That was diplomatic." Velma rested her hands on the counter, her fingers drumming out a light rhythm. "Tracy was always an independent person and I've been more of smotherer rather than a motherer." Velma clasped her hands together as if demonstrating. "It's always hard to let go."

"And she was sorry she missed you on Sunday." He made his voice casual, just a comment made in passing. But he figured she had to know.

Velma looked at him, her dark eyes, so much like Tracy's, holding a hint of puzzlement which slowly faded as she studied him. "You were the one in the truck, weren't you?"

"I drove her, yes." How would she know that if she wasn't home?

Velma acknowledged his comment with a nod. "I saw you drive up and drop her off. You and that little boy beside you. Tracy came to the door, took one look at me and left without saying one word." She looked down as she surreptitiously brushed her fingers over her eyes. "I was home all right."

David stared at her a moment, trying to fit her information in with what Tracy had told him. Velma couldn't be lying. How else would she have known that he had driven her and that Kent was with them?

David tried to ignore his own discomfort as he found a box of tissues and handed Velma one, puzzlement fighting with confusion and a measure of anger. He'd thought things were moving along between him and Tracy. In spite of the Heather fiasco, he'd thought he had earned her trust.

And now this?

"I'm sorry," Velma whispered, folding over the used tissue and dabbing once more at her eyes. "I've missed my little girl so much. I was looking forward to our visit all week." Velma looked up at David. "Did she give you a reason...?" She stopped and held her hand up in a negating gesture. "No. I'm sorry. Pretend I didn't ask that. It's none of my business."

She turned to leave.

"Wait. Don't go yet." David came around the counter, curiosity and concern propelling him. "Tracy didn't say anything to me about seeing you." He bit his lip, wondering if he should tell her. But if he wanted to find anything more about the puzzle that was Tracy, the woman standing in front of him was one large clue. "In fact, to be honest, Tracy said you weren't home."

Velma closed her eyes as if her daughter's denial was too much to bear. And David felt a stirring of sympathy for her.

"I know why Tracy said that." Velma's shoulders slumped as if in defeat. "I…the truth is…" Velma took a deep breath, then looked up at David, her eyes meeting his square on. "I haven't always been the mother I should for Tracy. I have…problems. But I have learned to depend on God." Velma gave a bitter laugh, then looked down at her intertwined hands. "I've made some horrible mistakes in the past. But I want to make things right."

She stopped then, her voice wavering.

David felt a surge of sympathy for this obviously broken woman. "Tracy was looking forward to seeing you on Sunday. I wish I could help you."

"You are very kind to me," she said softly. "As I said, I don't deserve her trust. Or her love."

"None of us deserve anything," David said. "But God gives us more than a second chance. I can try to talk to her. To convince her to give you another chance."

Velma gave David a shaky smile. "Thank you. I can't ask for more than that."

"If you had phoned, she might have been here," David offered.

"She must not answer her phone at night." Velma ran her fingers through her hair, rearranging the curls. "Thank you so much for your time, Dr. Braun. Please give Tracy my love. Tell her…" Velma hesitated, her hand toying with the lapel of her jacket, her smile tremulous "…tell her I love her. Tell her I forgive her. Tell her that I remember her in my prayers."

Velma looked so sad. She so obviously wanted a relationship with her daughter. He wanted to make things right between them. For Tracy as well as Velma.

"I'll tell her, Velma. And again, I'm sorry Tracy wasn't here."

Velma gave him another careful smile, then left. David walked to the window and watched as she got into a small, sporty car, pulled down the visor and checked her makeup. She wiped her eyes once more, then drove away.

Questions piled on top of questions. Why had Tracy lied to him about her visit to her mother? What was she trying to hide?

And what was he supposed to do with this information? In spite of his brave words to Velma, he didn't know if his relationship with Tracy was far enough along, strong enough for him to start giving her family advice.

Show me what to do, Lord. I care for her and want only what's best for her. And for her mother.

For now, all he could do was pray. And try to keep talking to Tracy. Keep being there for her, helping her to renew her relationship with her mother—hoping that one day she would trust him enough to tell him the truth.

"Administer one calcium bolus in about an hour. If she's not up by then, call me." David handed the package to Mrs. Swanson who nodded, and slipped it in the pocket of her blue jeans.

Tracy cleaned up the IV material, her eyes on the milk cow still lying on a bed of clean straw in a small barn, its breathing deep and heavy. Milk fever was easily treated, but tricky if not handled right. As always she was impressed with David's knowledge and his easy manner with the clients—four- and two-legged.

"That's a nice-looking animal," David was saying, drawing out a full-fledged smile from the usually taciturn Eva Swanson.

"She's quiet. Nice milker." Eva flexed her fingers as if demonstrating and Tracy had to smile. Not many farmers milked their cows by hand anymore, though according to Dr. Harvey it used to be more common.

"If you have any problems, don't hesitate to call," David said, taking the kit from Tracy.

They walked past a lean-to and Tracy glanced sideways at a shiny red car parked there. A faded for sale sign was tucked in the windshield.

"Is that your car?" she asked.

"Yeah. I've been tryin' to sell it, but no one 'round here wants it. Was gonna bring it to town, but never have time." Eva pushed her wobbly glasses up her nose with a thick forefinger. "It runs okay. I never had no worries with it." She hitched the waistband of her blue jeans above her ample waist and sniffed again. "Never did like that car."

"Is that the reason you're selling it?" Tracy asked.

Eva shrugged. Sniffed. "It's too small. Feel like my behind is draggin' on the road when I take it out. I prefer a truck."

David had popped the hood and was poking around

inside, tugging and shifting and doing engine-ly things that Tracy had no clue about.

"I got all my work done at Wierenga's in town." Eva scratched her hand, shifting her weight from one foot to the other, as if impatient for them to be gone. From the looks of the immaculate yard, she probably spent every waking hour clipping, weeding and cleaning. "You want it?"

David let the hood fall shut and glanced back at Tracy. She nodded. She wanted a vehicle. Didn't want to go to the auto lot in town. If the car was maintained as well as the yard was, it was probably very reliable.

"What do you want for it?" Tracy asked.

Eva waggled her hand, glancing from Tracy to David as if trying to figure out who was in charge. "Eight thousand?"

Eight thousand was probably about right, but the thought of taking that much money out of her savings account gave her a nervous shiver. That would mean that much less for her property. But she needed a car if she was going to be taking care of Kent.

She nodded, about to speak but David imperceptibly shook his head.

"The kilometers are a bit high for that price," David suggested, wiping his hands on a hanky.

"Seven?" Eva said, turning back to Tracy. But she was more than willing to let David do the haggling.

"It also looks like it's been in an accident," David continued.

"Hit a deer two weeks ago. 'Fore I bought the truck." Eva rubbed the side of her nose with her forefinger.

David only glanced back at the car, as if waiting for its side of the story.

"It still runs good," Eva added, her tone defensive.

David looked back at her, one eyebrow slightly raised. "Okay. Okay. Five and it's yours."

"Contingent on it passing a mechanical inspection."

Eva threw up her hands in surrender. "Fine. I'll get it into Wierenga's tomorrow. But we'll sign the bill of sale now. Drop the check off at Wierenga's if you think it's okay."

Ten minutes later they were back in the truck. "I would have settled for eight, you know," Tracy said, smiling at David.

"You probably didn't notice the corroded battery posts or the dent that had been pulled out in the passenger door."

"Nope. I'm strictly an I-come-I-see-I-buy shopper."

"It probably doesn't affect the condition of the car, but it definitely affects the resale value."

"Resale value is moot for me." She folded up the paper and slipped it into her pocket. "I only hope she agrees to stand by the deal."

David gave her a reassuring glance. "Eva comes across pretty gruff, but she's a woman of her word. She'll have that car at Wierenga's tomorrow."

"I know I can trust her. But my faith in humankind has taken a bit of a beating the past few days."

That was more than she wanted to divulge.

"Sometimes you just have to try again and give different people a chance to prove your opinion of the other ones wrong."

Tracy let the comment slip. Eva's coming through could hardly negate the anger and frustration of her mother's lapse. And what bothered her the most, was that it bothered her. She'd thought she had moved to a place in her life where she didn't need her mother as much.

Guess she was wrong.

"Kent will be happy," she said. "He's getting tired of walking to school."

"How was Kent's visit with his mother?" David asked.

"I guess she looked pretty bad from what he and the driver told me. I just wished they could have waited a bit, until she looked a little better."

"She probably missed him."

Tracy bit back her next comment. David knew too well her feelings toward Kent's mother. What he didn't know was that they were exactly the same feelings she had toward her own mother. And she didn't miss her mother.

"I know you don't agree with me on that, Tracy," David continued, as if able to read her thoughts, "but I do want to put in a plug for Kent's mom. She didn't ask to be put in the hospital."

"I know. But my priority is Kent." She didn't like hearing David defend Kent's mother. It was too short a step to defending her own. Time to change the subject. She looked away from him, out the window at the fields sliding past them.

A pair of combines were gobbling up swaths of barley, spewing out a cloud of straw and dust behind them. A truck paced one of the combines as golden grain poured out of the spout into the box.

She glanced sideways at David, surprised to see him looking at her, his hazel eyes like a gentle caress. It was a small miracle the way her smile drew an answering one from him. A response. It seemed she was forgiven.

"By the way, thanks for helping me with the car." Tracy asked, moving a little closer to David. Staking out her fragile territory, she draped her arm across the back of the truck's seat. "I'm not very good at dealing."

"Who helped you with your last car?"

"Danielle's brother."

"She has three brothers, doesn't she?"

"Two older, one younger and the worst collection of *guys* on the face of the planet."

"Guys?"

"Danielle always says her brothers aren't men, they're guys."

"What's the difference?"

"Men like challenges that stretch their intellect. Guys like meaningless challenges that usually involve pain. Men like to fix things. Guys like taking things apart to see how they work. And then leaving the parts around." She laid her hand on his shoulder, just because she could, rested her fingers against his warm neck, making a physical connection with him. Took a chance on a tiny bit of disclosure. "Art was a guy. You're not."

His laugh made her feel like she was actually funny, instead of slightly cynical. Then he turned his attention back to the road. He grew silent, his forehead puckered in concentration as he drove. The silence didn't bother her. Tracy was content just to look. To know that she could.

He had strong features. Large deep eyes, well-defined nose, firm lips. The kind of face that would grow more appealing with age and time spent together. She allowed herself a bit of dreaming. A moment of wondering where this relationship was going.

If there was a future. An "us."

His frown deepened as his gaze snagged hers. "What?"

Tracy took another chance and let her index finger trickle down his neck, her knuckle grazing the rough hairs on his neck. "Nothing. I guess I just like looking at you."

"Considering what you have to look at, I'm thankful for small blessings." He caught her other hand in his and held it tightly.

"You're a blessing, David." He was dependable. Loving. And before she could analyze or think, she spoke. "And I think…"

She stopped. Was it too soon? She felt as if she was teetering on the edge of a place she'd been before. Did she dare fall again?

Say it. Don't wait. David was worth taking a chance on.

"…and I think…"

He glanced at her, expectation in his eyes.

"I really care for you."

Chapter Thirteen

Lame. Lame, Tracy. You choked. Why couldn't you tell him?

Then, to her surprise, David's hand tightened on hers, and, without warning, he pulled the truck to the side of the road, hit the brakes and pulled her into his arms.

Then his mouth was on hers, calling out a response, drawing forth a flurry of emotions, of hope.

It had happened so fast, she didn't have time to shore up her defenses.

And as she slipped her arms around him, she knew she didn't want to.

In one smooth motion, David slipped the truck into Park and turned back to her. His sigh brushed her cheek as his lips grazed hers. He cupped her cheeks in his hands, his eyes holding hers with an intensity she had never seen before. "I wanted to tell you before, but I didn't dare. I care for you too. In fact, Tracy, I love you."

She clung to him and pressed her face into his

sweater. Why did she suddenly feel her throat thicken? Why did she feel like laughing and crying at the same time? She had pulled back, and instead of allowing her to withdraw, he had given her all of this.

David stroked her hair, murmured something unintelligible, his voice soothing as her emotions stabilized.

She lifted her face to his. His mouth was close to hers so she kissed him, wonder and love spiraling through her. "You love me?"

She had to repeat his words, as if by doing so, she made them more real.

"I do," he said with a grin. "Haven't been quite able to figure out the whys and wherefores but I don't know if love works like that." He traced the line of her brow, ran his finger lightly down her nose. "I just know that with you I feel complete. Whole. Alive."

She bit her lip at his declaration.

Tell him. Tell him. You know you love him too.

"I wish I could think of something poetic," she said with a self-deprecating laugh, pushing aside the dangerous urge. "Something I can put in my journal."

"I didn't know you kept a journal."

"I keep a lot of things. Old shoes. Single mittens. Grudges."

David laughed again, as he leaned back, his rough finger tracing the curve of her ear. "Those are hard to get rid of."

"I've tried. But no one wants them." She sighed lightly. "I know I can give them over to God, but I have a hard time letting go."

His finger slowed. Came to rest at her neck as his

expression grew serious. "What kind of grudges do you hold?"

She hesitated, wondering if she should go for the joke, or let this be a moment of revelation. He had just told her he loved her even though she hadn't returned the declaration. She owed him more than a glib comment.

"I have a lot of resentment with my mother."

"Was that why it was so hard to make the decision to visit her?"

Tracy nodded, wondering how much farther to go. "There's a lot of stuff, history between us. I wanted to see her, yet…"

"Is that why you didn't?"

Tracy's heart jumped. "What do you mean?"

David stroked her neck lightly, his gaze on his fingers, avoiding hers. "I didn't have a chance to tell you until now, but your mother came by on Monday afternoon. When you were gone."

Oh no. Was she drunk?

"What did she want?"

"To see you. To find out why you didn't stay on Sunday." His deep voice was quiet, but Tracy heard a faint condemnation in it. He pulled his lower lip between his teeth, then looked directly at her, his gaze almost piercing.

Please, Lord, she thought. *Not this. Not from David.*

She folded her arms across her chest. So now what? Tell him the truth? Watch him run the way Art had? Or introduce the serpent of a lie into their still-fragile relationship and be forever trying to make sure he never found out?

"What did she tell you?" She wasn't going to defend herself. Wasn't going to reveal more than she had to until she had no other option.

David slipped his hand around her neck, as if ignoring her retreat. "She told me that she wanted a relationship with you. And she seemed very sad."

Tracy closed her eyes, focusing inward. She didn't want to hear sympathy for her mother in David's voice. He was supposed to be on her side.

"She told me that she wants to change," he continued. "That she's been trusting in God to help her with her struggles."

Tracy pressed her fingers against her eyes. Why wasn't she surprised? Her charming mother was always one step ahead of her. One step ahead of well-meaning neighbors who heard Tracy's side of the story, who saw her alone so often. One step ahead of teachers, social workers and anyone with authority who sensed a problem and wanted to help.

The only struggle her mother had was trying to find someone to pay for her drinking.

"Did she cry?" Tracy asked, unable to keep the bitterness out of her voice.

"As a matter of fact, she did."

"She's good at that." Tracy looked up at David as the first chill of fury crept around her consciousness. "I used to envy her ability to cry on command, drunk or sober." She didn't mean to come across as unfeeling and harsh. But the surprise on David's face showed her she had done exactly that.

"I think she was sincere." David moved across the

seat, drew Tracy's hands into his own. "She said she misses you."

Tracy looked down at his fingers with their blunt tips, the long white scar that ran down from his thumb to his wrist. He'd told her he'd gotten it when he and a friend were playing soldiers with his mother's steak knives. When he'd come stumbling into the kitchen, blood pouring from his hand, his mother had nearly fainted. Still feeling shaky, she had driven him to the hospital weaving all over the road. David chuckled when he'd told her, saying that his mother's driving scared him far more than the cut had.

When he'd told her that story, it was with a sense of expectation—as if it was now her turn to tell him something from her childhood.

Tracy had stories quite similar to David's. Only her mother's erratic driving was because she was drunk. Not the kind of thing she wanted to share. Any other stories were best left where they were. She'd pushed them into the past and they were better left there. It was the only way she knew of keeping herself from becoming bitter.

"You don't have other family, do you?" he pressed.

"Not that I'm aware of." Tracy aimed for a light tone. Tried to move away from the dark place of her childhood.

"No grandparents. Uncles?"

Why was he pushing so hard? She didn't want to talk about the past. When a man and a woman expressed their love for each other, there were better things to discuss. Future things.

The earnestness of his gaze pulled a reluctant confession from her. "My mother's parents disowned her, and my mother didn't even really know who my father was. Not for certain anyhow." What a legacy. With each sentence, each question, the difference between her and Heather was growing more pronounced. And she was coming off very badly indeed. She forced a light laugh. "Can we please not talk about my mother? Or my lack of family? It's…well, a painful subject." The comment sounded slick and insincere, but she had to keep him away from her past. Had to keep herself away from it as well.

"I know so little about you, Tracy. You don't tell me much."

"I just need some time, okay?"

"You can trust me, you know."

As she held his sincere gaze, she knew it was true.

"Then trust me to tell you that my life was not pretty. My mother was an alcoholic. She was gone a lot. She was drunk a lot." Tracy took a deep breath. *Please Lord, help me through this.* "There are times I miss her, but mostly I truly…" She paused thinking of Heather. Perfect, loving, Christian Heather. But he had to know. "There were…are…many times that I wish she were dead. There were many times I used to imagine myself as an orphan. Still do. Because then I wouldn't have to deal with her coming in and out of my life. Making me hope that this time it would be different. I didn't have a cozy childhood with parents and family. I spent a lot of time alone. Afraid. And whenever I tried to tell anyone what my life was like, they would talk to my mother and she could charm their concerns away. Of course I can hardly blame those people. I was charmed by her too. And again and again I gave her another chance. That Sunday you took me to Kolvik, she showed up at the door, drunk. Another broken promise. I am not going to let her do that to me again. If I do, then I'm the idiot, aren't I?"

David closed his eyes, as if denying what she had to say. She bit her lip. Looked away.

The high-pitched warble of his cell phone was her deliverance. But he ignored it.

"You should get that," she said, still looking sightlessly out the window.

He waited as it rang again, but shame kept her eyes averted.

She listened to his deep voice speaking curtly to whoever had called. He sounded angry, and she was to blame.

But what else could she do? Surely he would understand that she couldn't let her mother hurt her again. She had given everything she could.

Seventy times seven?

Oh, Lord, please, she prayed. *I'm sure I'm up to at least four hundred. I'm imperfect. Sinful. And I can't absorb ninety more disappointments.*

David shut his cell phone and dropped it on the seat beside him. Without saying anything to Tracy, he put the truck into gear and pulled back onto the highway.

The trip to the clinic was quick and silent. Tracy kept her face to the window, resentment slowly burning within her.

You did it again, Mom. Once again you've come between me and a man I love.

Her heart stuttered as hot tears gathered at the back of her throat.

Though she had fought it, she knew she was falling in love with David after all. And, thanks to her mother, David had got to see exactly what kind of unforgiving woman she really was.

When they got to the clinic, she barely gave David time to stop the truck, trying to get out as quickly as possible, but David caught her by the arm. "I'm sorry, Tracy," he said. "I was out of line. Please forgive me."

Tracy turned to him, taken aback first by his apology and secondly by the sad look on his face.

"I'm sorry. For pushing you. It was just that…" He reluctantly let go of her. "I feel like it's taking too long to get to know you."

"There's not a statute of limitations on this," she said quietly, his apology giving her the courage to look directly at him. "We won't run out of time."

"I don't know about that."

His soft reply caught her unawares. And she realized he was talking about his relationship with Heather.

She couldn't say anything right then, but she didn't want to leave either. Not like this. So she closed the door. Let David pull her to his side. And she rested against him, the security of his arms surrounding her.

He sighed lightly, his breath warm on the top of her head. "I want you to be happy."

"You make me happy." She laid her hand against his chest, feeling the steady thump of his heart under her fingers. A heart that he had given to her. "I don't need much more than that."

Please Lord, let him be content with that.

His chest lifted in a long, slow sigh and then, to her surprise he kissed the top of her head. "Then that's where we'll leave it."

"And how do you work at resolving problems?" Phillip Measures clicked his pen again, his head bent over the ten-page form lying on Tracy's table.

She glanced over at Kent, who lay on his stomach, his chin in his hands as he stared at the television. She hated parking him in front of the TV like this, but until she was done with Mr. Measures she had no choice.

"Miss Harris?" Philip prompted.

"Sorry. Just checking on Kent." Her excuse for her distraction gave her the added benefit of sounding concerned. "I come across problems every day in my work," she answered, focusing her attention on the paper in front of Phillip. "I usually pull back from the emotions of the situation and look at my options. Change the things I can and adjust to cope with the things that I can't, or I try to find innovative solutions that will result in a harmonious situation." She sat back, and folded her arms across her chest, well-satisfied with the bafflegab she was spewing.

And how did you apply that to your particular problem with your mother?

The faintly accusing inner voice slipped past her veneer of self-satisfaction.

But I did follow my own advice, she countered. My mother won't change. I adjusted to cope with it by deciding not to let her be a part of my life. After all I have Kent to think of now.

Phillip nodded. Clicked his pen six more times. "I think we've covered most of that section," he said, flipping the paper over.

Tracy glanced at the remaining papers. Two more. In about ten minutes Kent would be bored and would come into the kitchen to pester her and Phillip. She hoped they were done before that happened.

"We're going to talk now about support systems." Click. Click. Click. "Foster parents are under an enormous amount of stress. Stress from the children and from the natural parents. What I'd like to know is what kind of support you have in place."

Tracy leaned back, her mind suddenly blank. This is where most people would say parents, spouses, kids, that kind of thing.

"Well, I have a very close relationship with Danielle, her father and her brothers." Even though they were guys, they were still supportive. "As a teen I spent a lot of time there."

Phillip frowned. "Why was that?"

"My mother was gone a lot. When I was alone, Alice became my second mother, the Hemstead home my second home."

"I see."

And what, Tracy wondered, did he see? And why was it that her mother was now popping up in every aspect of her life when Velma had spent so many years blissfully unaware of Tracy's very existence?

"Danielle is my best friend," Tracy continued. "In the time she has worked with child welfare I've grown aware of what she has had to deal with both with foster parents and with natural parents. She is someone I can depend on for help."

She gave Phillip a chance to write that down. "I belong to a strong church community. I know that if I have any problems, I can turn either to my pastor, my fellow church members or…" She hesitated, feeling self-conscious. She didn't often speak openly about her faith so this was a little harder.

"Or…" Phillip prompted.

"Or I pray about my problems. Bring them before the Lord."

Phillip darted her a quizzical look, which wasn't reassuring. Should she have said that?

"I depend on my Lord for strength," she said, speaking the words aloud with renewed conviction and determination. "He has given me so much. And I want to share that with Kent." She crossed her arms, trying to still the flutters in her stomach. Yet a deep peace slipped through her, calming her. To minimize her faith would be to minimize God's love for her. And to minimize her dependance on God would be more pride than she dared indulge in.

Thankfully, she watched Phillip give her a careful smile. "That's good." He looked back down at the paper. "And your parents. I take it they are deceased?"

"No. My mother is still alive."

"What is your relationship like?"

Tracy blinked, taken aback by this line of questioning. She thought she had deflected him from her mother but obviously not.

"Is this important?"

"It's not essential, but it is part of the information I need to gather from you."

Tracy took a deep breath, reminding herself that he was just doing his job. "My mother and I have a complex relationship. She wasn't very supportive when I was younger." Translation—not around. "I haven't seen her for a while, though she has just moved back to Kolvik. I don't see that as relevant."

Phillip just shrugged. "Maybe not." He wrote something down, but Tracy couldn't read his handwriting.

"She's not really a part of my life. I mean, she has had a few problems, but I'm thankful I've overcome that."

And if she didn't stop talking she'd be giving him a play by play of a typical evening in the Harris household after one of Velma's many drinking binges.

You're not a criminal, Tracy reminded herself, pressing her arms tighter against her chest as Phillip clicked and wrote. You're not on trial. It's just a bunch of questions. Formality.

But it still brought out a latent anger with her mother, and, as she looked at Kent, who was giggling at the cartoon he was watching, with Kent's mother.

"Would you have a problem working with Kent's mother?"

"Yes I would." The answer had jumped out of her mouth before she realized what she was saying.

Wrong. Wrong. Wrong.

"I mean, I wouldn't normally," she amended hastily, her thoughts and words tripping over themselves in her rush to clarify. "Though right now his mother is in the hospital, so of course that would be a problem. I mean a problem in terms of working with her." Oh boy. This was getting worse.

Phillip just nodded and wrote and Tracy slumped down in her chair.

She had to learn to separate her disappointment with her own mother from her disappointment with Kent's mother. It was just so hard.

"And you are employed full-time?"

This was more neutral territory. "I work at the vet clinic. I've supplied my bosses there as a reference."

"And you understand you'll have to undergo a criminal-record check?"

"Yes."

Phillip folded the last of the papers over and tucked his pen into his pocket. He glanced over at Tracy, giving her a quick smile as he got up. "I'll pass this on to Danielle and we'll let you know what happens."

She returned his handshake, gave him what she hoped was an appropriate smile. As soon as the door closed behind him, she dropped against it, her bones feeling like overcooked spaghetti.

It was done. She had said what she could. The rest she'd have to leave in God's hands.

Chapter Fourteen

"Do you remember what our waitress said about the specials?"

David glanced at his watch. "On Thursday, it's tomato and rice soup with chicken quiche." He caught Tracy's puzzled glance and shrugged. "I eat here a lot, okay?"

"I'll start worrying about you when you get your own table like the retired farmers over there." Tracy hitched her thumb over her shoulder at a booth in the far corner of the restaurant where a group of older men sat in a haze of cigarette smoke, each nursing a cup of coffee.

It was early afternoon and they were killing time between a difficult caesarean section on a Holstein cow and their appointment with Danielle to discuss Kent's case and his future. Tracy was nervous. When David had suggested lunch, the only thing that made her agree was the idea of catching a little bit of private time with him, something Tracy found she couldn't get enough of with David.

Every day they spent together, every conversation, proved again that what she shared with David was much more than she ever had with Art. The thought made her both immensely happy and immensely frightened.

Vulnerable again.

She looked at David, smiling as his eyes caught hers. It was different with David. He was the kind of man who would be there for her.

"And how do you know about the geezer guys?" David said with a grin.

"David! Have some respect!" Tracy pretended to look shocked. "Those men have inhabited that space since the first day Dani and I were brave enough to skip school and come here."

"You skipped classes?" David heaved an exaggerated sigh. "And you dare to accuse me of being disrespectful? Talk about your double standard."

"Skipping class is expected of high-school students." Tracy's attention was caught by a gaggle of teens clustered around a table, talking too loudly, laughing too hard, all hoping to be the center of attention rather than the loser on the outskirts. "And you could never accuse the two of us of not meeting expectations."

"Danielle is a good friend, isn't she?"

"My best. I spent more time at her place than I did at my own."

David rested his elbows on the table, his movement towards her creating a circle of intimacy. He reached across the table. Took her hand in his as his expression grew serious. "I want you to know that you matter a lot to me. More than anyone has before."

She gave a nervous laugh. "This sounds a little ominous."

David ran his rough fingers over hers. "It isn't. Not really. But before we go to the meeting with Danielle, I just want to…" He hesitated, kept his eyes averted from hers. "Well, explain a few things."

Tracy swallowed. Tried to pull her hand away just in case he was going to tell her something bad. Something like, "I found out that your mother is a crazy alcoholic and I don't want to see you anymore."

Focus, Tracy. Not everything in your life is about your mother.

"So. Here you are." A shadow fell across the table. Stifling a light sigh, Tracy looked up.

Edgar Stinson stood beside them, his arms folded across his chest, his greasy cap pulled low over his eyes. His timing couldn't be worse.

"Where's my grandson?" Edgar's narrow eyes held hers, waves of intimidation washing over her.

"Pardon me?" David asked, still holding Tracy's hand. She was thankful for an anchor in a suddenly topsy-turvy moment.

"I'm looking for that Kent boy." Edgar's gaze flicked to David, then back to Tracy, as if he knew she was the one he could bully. "He's not with his mother in his apartment."

Because his mother was in the hospital.

"We're not going to discuss that with you," David said.

Tracy gave him a grateful look. Squeezed his hand harder.

"You better. He's my grandson."

"Kent is not your grandson," Tracy said, finally finding her voice, though she wished she sounded more confident. Standing up to Edgar Stinson, after months of careful treatment of him was a new thing for her. And dangerous ground to be walking on. "There's no proof at all that he's related to you."

"You sound pretty sure 'bout that." Edgar gave her a half smile that slithered through Tracy's midsection. "Well, so am I. Did you notice a spot on his back? Shaped like an egg?"

Tracy did remember. Had seen it whenever she bathed and dressed the little boy. How would Edgar know about it? Lucky guess?

Edgar's nasty smile grew tight, as if he had heard her silent question. "I seen it couple of times when he was a baby. When his mom came to our house. Seems she was pretty anxious then for my Steve to claim him."

Denial spun through Tracy. She didn't want to hear this. Didn't want to know that Edgar was more connected to that precious little boy than she was.

Edgar laid his oil-grimed hands on the table and leaned closer to Tracy, invading her personal space, his eyes burning into hers like a laser.

"Excuse me, Mr. Stinson. I don't think Tracy wants to talk to you right now." Dear David. Tracy was so glad he was there.

Edgar kept his cold eyes on Tracy, his smile growing. "I think this little lady does. And you know why? I think she wants to talk if she wants to keep that acreage she's been pestering me about."

Tracy just stared as the sinister meaning of his words

sank in. "What are you talking about?" Panic crept along the edges of her thoughts, waiting for the implied threat to fall.

Edgar's smile dropped away. "You stay away from my grandson. And his mom. Or you're going to lose that acreage."

He *was* going to do it.

The panic jumped and rushed into her mind. Followed closely by oily fear. Stay calm. Don't be bullied.

"Tracy…" David said, but Tracy shook her head.

"I'll take care of this," she said. She turned back to Edgar. She had to do this on her own. "We signed an agreement on that land, Edgar. You have a thousand dollars for the subdivision. The deal has nothing to do with Kent whether he's your grandchild or not."

Edgar laughed shortly. "But it does, missy. I can tear up that agreement. It won't mean nothing."

"Tracy has a signed copy of the agreement," David said.

Edgar shook his head as if dealing with a particularly stupid child. "I talked to my lawyer about that. Said that according to some law, the person who draws up the agreement is the one who hasta make it clear." He turned his icy gaze back to Tracy. "I don't think it's clear, I don't have to 'bide by it."

"You agreed to sell it to me." Couldn't she come up with anything more substantial than that?

He shrugged, his coat riding up. "And I will. You get that social worker off his case. Let my Steve take care of him."

"We can't do that. Kent's mother is his legal guardian." At least until Danielle set up her case. Which they were going to be discussing in just a few minutes.

Edgar shrugged her comments away. "She's not capable of carin' for him. I am. Now, you stay away from that boy or lose the land."

Tracy's panicked gaze flitted to David. He shook his head imperceptibly. She felt his strength seep from his warm fingers into her. And she looked back at Edgar.

"Why are you doing this?"

"We Stinsons take care of our own. That's all." He didn't budge. Didn't let his gaze so much as flicker.

Fear clawed at Tracy, pulling down her defenses. You'll lose the land. Your dream.

He's just a bully. He's just making noise. You've stood up to him before, you can do it again.

The memory of Kent's fear around David, around "Uncle Steve" solidified her resolve.

"Sorry, Mr. Stinson. I love Kent and I'm going to do what's best for him. And that means I'm going to take care of him." She looked him in the eye. "Our agreement should have nothing to do with Kent. And if you care for him, you'll want what's best for him as well."

Edgar held her gaze a moment, as if testing her resolve. Then, with a snort, he pulled some folded-over papers out of his pocket and threw them on the table. "The deal is over, missy. You lost your land."

And then he left.

Tracy's breath felt as if it had been sucked away with his leaving. All she heard play over and over again was, *You lost your land.*

It was over. Her dream of the past few years was dead.

Ice pooled in her chest, then seeped out into her blood, chilling her arms, her hands. Now what?

Dimly she became aware of David's warm fingers wrapped around her hand, as if pulling her back.

"Hey, Tracy. Are you okay?"

Cold fingers gripped her temples as she slowly turned back to David. His hazel eyes, warm with concern, held hers. He'd seen it all. Seen her humiliation. Her disappointment.

She clung to him with one hand while she reassembled the papers Edgar had tossed in front of her.

It was the agreement. At the bottom, Edgar had crossed out his signature in bold red strokes and had written Invalid underneath.

She closed her eyes, pulling herself down to the quiet center she would retreat to at other, dark times of her life. Times when her mother was stumbling around the apartment, calling her stupid and useless. When her mother's equally drunk boyfriend of the moment would yell at them both. And the even harder times when no one was yelling at anyone because she was all alone.

This isn't fair, Lord. I didn't ask for this. I don't deserve this. I've done whatever I could. Was this small dream so much to wish for? To ask for?

She kept her eyes fixed unseeingly on the paper as she pulled her hand out of David's and wrapped her arms around her waist, holding in the pain. But what else could she do? She wasn't going to give up Kent for some land.

But, oh, how it hurt.

Then David was beside her, his arm over her shoulder.

Her first reaction was to retreat. To find a quiet place to lick her wounds. To regain her strength. But from here she had to go to the meeting about Kent.

Where his future would be decided.

"It's okay, Tracy," David said, still holding her, ignoring the stiffness of her body. "He signed the agreement. I witnessed it. We'll get through this."

It was the *we* that melted her resistance, warmed her cold soul. And with a light sigh, she leaned against him, let his strength hold her up.

She rested her hand on his broad chest. Just for a moment.

"I'm glad you were here, David," she said softly.

"Me too," he whispered, brushing a light kiss over her forehead.

She drew in a long, slow breath and pulled away. "I don't want anything to eat," she said. "Can we go?"

"Sure." He slipped out of the booth, standing aside to let her get up. His hand at her back was a gentle support as they walked out. She didn't know if she could have made it alone.

"Do you want me to drive you to the meeting?" David asked as they walked across the parking lot to their vehicles. A cool wind sifted around them, pulling away what little warmth Tracy had left in her body.

"I think I'll take my car, thanks."

He put his forefinger under her chin and gently lifted it. His eyes held hers with an intensity that kindled her own love, then he bent down, brushed a kiss over her lips. "This isn't over yet."

"Thanks, David," she said, cupping his warm face in her chilled hand, her emotions still in turmoil. She smiled. Then dared some more. "I love you."

He caught her hands, squeezing them so tightly he almost hurt her. "Oh, Tracy. I wish…." He bit his lips, then gave her a quick kiss. "No matter what happens, I want you to know that I love you too. More than I've ever cared for anyone." His gaze bored into hers, as if underlining his words, and Tracy felt a vague premonition of fear. "Always remember."

"I will," she said, puzzled at his intensity.

"I'll see you at the meeting." He gave her another quick kiss and then strode toward his truck.

Tracy glanced down at the paper, then pushed it back into her purse. She had made the right decision. She could go through this with David's love.

Okay, Lord. This is it. Help me say the right thing. Tracy took another quick look at herself in the rearview mirror of her car. Licked her lips once more and pressed her hand to her pounding heart. A heart that already felt bruised, but that still had so much on the line. Her dream had been snatched away and, in spite of David's brave words, she didn't think she had any chance of seeing it back.

She had given up a chance on her dream for Kent's sake. Which now meant that she didn't have the acreage she had told social services she would be moving to. Kent wouldn't have the home she had hoped to provide for him.

Please, Lord. Don't let that make a difference. Don't

let them turn me down because of it. I can give this boy a lot.

And she had David. She had told him she loved him. Had made that huge step into the unknown of trusting him.

In spite of her raging disappointment, she felt a warm glow wrap itself around her heart.

David loved her.

God loved her.

Kent loved her.

Please Lord. I want to take care of him. I want to be the mother he doesn't have.

She held the thought a moment, as if holding on to Kent. Then, with a hesitating heart, she prayed another prayer.

I want what's best for him.

She pressed her lips together, grabbed her purse and stepped out of her car into the brisk fall morning. Enough thinking. It was time.

And as she walked down the long hallway to the meeting room, she wished Danielle could have done this over the phone rather than make this an official meeting. A case conference, no less.

"Hey, Tracy. You're the first one." Danielle looked up from the papers she was assembling on a long table. Her smile was offset by her I-mean-business suit: a navy-blue blazer with a high collar and matching narrow skirt. This was the suit she wore to court dates and business meetings. It was as austere as the room.

A sliver of panic born of her momentary vulnerability and the faint chill of the room wedged into Tracy's mind. The rustling of Danielle's papers echoed as she slipped them into a file folder and closed it.

"Who else is going to be here?" Tracy asked, glancing around the government-issue room. An easel stood at one end of the table. Metal chairs with padded seats were scattered along each side.

Cold. Unfeeling. Unwelcoming.

She had hoped David would be here by now. He had been right behind her when they'd left the parking lot of the inn.

"David, of course. And Juanita's caseworker, Oden Holmgren." Danielle moved the file over one inch. "I also got a call from Emily and Jack Friedman. They are foster parents as well and were also interested in Kent's case."

Tracy frowned. "What is this. An auction?"

Danielle walked around the table, her hand reaching out to Tracy. "No. It's just a group of people interested in Kent's well-being."

How would Emily and Jack have known about this? David?

Tracy pushed the thought aside. David knew how much she loved Kent. He wouldn't sabotage her situation. Emily and Jack were foster parents. They probably had their own information network.

The door squeaked open. Tracy glanced backward, pleased to see David step into the room. An ally.

Then, right behind him came Emily and Jack.

David walked to Tracy's side, his expression unreadable. Tracy looked back to Danielle, who was fussing with some papers.

And a sick dread spiraled through her.

She brushed past David. Pulled the chair back from

the table and sat. She twined her fingers through each other, vague fears chasing each other, unformed and frightening.

Relax, she warned herself. You don't know what this is about. Kent has been staying with you. You're the one who told Danielle about him. You've prayed and prayed about it. Let it go.

She repeated the phrases as David sat beside her, Emily and Jack across from her. As they waited for Oden, she kept her attention focused on her bloodless hands. By the time he came, Tracy's feet were chilled with a cold sweat and her stomach was a tight knot.

Danielle's introductions barely registered. She only glanced at Oden Holmgren, out of politeness, she couldn't do much more than that.

Give us this day our daily bread. Help me to trust in You, Lord. You are faithful and loving. You know what's best for Kent.

"Of course our first priority in this situation is Kent's well-being," Danielle was saying after the introductions. "Our second is the relationship with Kent's mother, Juanita."

Tracy blew out her breath, pulled in another. Looked up at Danielle.

Danielle balanced a pen between her hands as her gaze flicked over the people gathered around the table. "Juanita told me the nearest family she has is a father who, at the moment, is imprisoned in Quebec."

"Juanita did mention her father," Oden said. "She stated unequivocally that her family was in no way a consideration. She has a sister and a grandmother both of whom reside in the Maritimes. Too far away to be considered either."

A gentle calm settled on Tracy as she saw other possibilities slowly get removed. Just Jack and Emily remained.

"And the boy's father?" David asked, his eyes fixed on Danielle.

"Juanita won't name him, though I did get a phone call from Edgar Stinson claiming to be the boy's grandfather. We're not pursuing that angle."

Relief sluiced through Tracy. That particular avenue was closed.

Danielle turned to her. "Tracy, I was wondering if you could give us your view of Kent's condition right now?"

Tracy smiled at Danielle, pleased at the recognition. "Kent is settling nicely into my home. He misses his mother, but the visits to the hospital have helped." David sat askew on his chair, but his eyes were on the paper in front of him. She couldn't look at Emily and Jack. Didn't want to acknowledge them or even wonder what they were here for. "He's a bright little boy and I've become extremely fond of him."

"I understand you live in a one-bedroom apartment," Oden was saying, leaning forward into her view.

Tracy only nodded, swallowing down an unwelcome knot of pain and anger. Half an hour ago she would have been able to lay out her future plans. Her house. The wonderful open spaces that Kent would be able to play in.

"And this is important because…" David asked, arching an eyebrow at the caseworker.

"I'm speaking on behalf of Juanita, who also wants the best for Kent," Oden said quietly.

"He lived in an apartment with his mother," Tracy snapped, her anger spilling out. "It wasn't a problem then."

"*With his mother* being the operative words," Oden replied.

"I believe I can give Kent what he needs," Tracy said.

"Tracy was the one who was involved with him before his mother disappeared," Danielle broke in, her eyes on Oden. "And she was the one who filed the initial report."

First David, now Danielle, Tracy thought, relaxing ever so slightly back into her chair. She wasn't alone after all.

Danielle opened the file folder in front of her. "Now we need to decide what we can do for both Kent and his mother that will give them the help and support they need to maintain their relationship."

"Juanita will be released from the hospital tomorrow," Oden said. "I can't see why Kent cannot be put back into her care."

"I've done some research into Juanita and Kent's background," Danielle said, pulling out another piece of paper. "There have been reports of neglect in other places they've lived. And while they've been living here, Tracy has reported a few alarming situations concerning Kent to me previous to Juanita being in the hospital. At the moment, the landlord has served an eviction notice, so she technically has no place to live. You've got a copy of that report, Oden?" He nodded.

"I talked to Juanita and laid out her options, and she's amenable to a custody agreement cooperating with the conditions we agreed on."

"And what are the conditions?" David asked Danielle.

Danielle's teeth worried one corner of her lip and Tracy held her breath. "I think Oden will be speaking to that," Danielle said, her entire attention focused on the open file in front of her as she spoke.

"We want to see Kent in a safe, loving environment first of all," Oden said.

My home, thought Tracy.

"We want a situation where he has a positive male role model."

David could be that.

"We'd like to see Juanita coming for regular visits."

Tracy felt a glimmer of foreboding.

"I'd like to see her understand how a family functions. I want *her* to have a role model in that area as well."

Tracy closed her eyes, bracing for her second hit of the day.

"So what I propose is that Juanita sign a voluntary three-month custody agreement, and we place Kent in Jack and Emily Friedman's home for the duration of that agreement. Starting today."

Chapter Fifteen

Oden's words hit Tracy like a body blow. She fell back against her chair, anger and fear swirling through her.

No. *Dear Lord, this can't be.*

Danielle's gaze flew to hers and Tracy realized she had cried out.

David's hand cupped her shoulder. Jack and Emily just looked down.

Tracy held Danielle's gaze, pleading silently with her. But Danielle only looked away.

She turned back to David. The man who had said he loved her. "David. You know how much I love Kent. What I've done for him." He'd been there when she'd sacrificed her chance at a dream she'd had longer than she'd had Kent. He'd seen the choice she made. "You know this isn't right."

David squeezed harder. "I know this is hard, Tracy. But we've got to think about Kent."

"And what about me?"

"I have thought about you. So has Danielle. Your problems with your mother make it hard to see you working with Juanita."

"My mother?" Tracy's gaze flew from David to Danielle then back again. "My mother has nothing to do with this. Nothing at all."

Surely she wasn't going to be penalized for what she had told him? For what she had confessed to him. "What I told you, I told you in confidence…" She paused, gasping for breath, her heart pounding. "This is what I get?"

"You misunderstand, Tracy. It's not that. We want Kent to be in the best place possible…" David's glance slipped to Emily and Jack, and in a flash Tracy understood.

Heather's perfect family. So much better than what she could give Kent.

David had betrayed her. Just as her mother had. Just as Art had. How could she have been so stupid as to believe he would take care of her? How could she have trusted him with secrets she had never told anyone before?

The walls of the room closed in on her. She had to get out.

Tracy slapped David's hand away, pushed her chair back, the legs catching on the carpet. She tried to get up, but her knees buckled and David caught her.

She looked at him, saw the pity in his gaze.

"You knew," she said, clinging a moment to catch her balance. "Before we came here, you knew what was going to happen."

"Tracy, I can explain."

"I don't need your lame explanations," she cried out,

pushing him away. "You leave me alone. I don't want your pity. Or your help."

She snatched her purse from the back of her chair. Made it to the door without stumbling.

"Tracy, wait," David called out.

"Stay away from me, David. Just stay away."

As the door slammed behind her she looked wildly around for escape. A large square of light at the end of the hallway beckoned and she ran blindly toward it, hoping, praying David wasn't following her.

She slammed her hands against the metal bars, startling a young couple entering the building. With a mumbled apology she ran past them, floundered down the concrete stairs, thankful she was staying on her feet.

She stopped a moment, uncertain of where to go. The wind had died down, giving the sun a chance to give off what little heat it had at this time of the year. But Tracy shivered as the full import of what had just happened fell on her, an avalanche of broken wishes and dreams.

Kent wasn't going to be staying with her.

Her dream acreage had been taken away from her.

She had sacrificed it for Kent. Had sacrificed it for nothing.

She swayed as pain clawed at her heart, sharp, hard, unyielding and unrelenting. Sanctuary. She needed sanctuary.

But the two people she trusted the most, the ones she'd thought cared about her, were huddled in a room in the building behind her, making plans for a little boy she had dared let into her life and heart because she foolishly thought he couldn't break it.

Unworthy. Unworthy.

The word spun around her head, condemning. Accusing.

It was because of her mother. Because of her unyielding resistance to reconcile with a woman she didn't dare allow into her life.

She had kept her mother away because she thought that could keep her from being hurt. But it was that rejection that had jeopardized her chance to take care of Kent.

She swallowed and swallowed, determined not to cry. Tears were futile. They solved nothing. But as she walked toward her car she tasted salt at the corners of her mouth, felt the cool tracks of moisture trickling down her cheeks.

She unlocked her car with shaking fingers, got inside, and carefully slid the key into the ignition. But she didn't have the strength to turn it.

Bewildered, she lifted her hands as if to inspect them. Her vision blurred, the stone that was her heart grew heavier and heavier in her chest, pressing on the sorrow she tried to hold in.

She clenched her hands into fists, pressed them against each other as she rocked in her seat. Then, unable to hold it in any longer, she opened her hands, pressed them to her face and wept.

Kent was gone. Taken away. Her little boy whom she had dared to love.

David, the man she had given her heart to, had betrayed her.

She had no dreams. No hope. No future.

Only a mother who had once again torn everything away from her.

Oh God, what have I done to deserve this?

Tracy stacked her hands on the steering wheel. Laid her forehead on them and closed her eyes.

Slowly, coherent thought slipped past the pain. Now what? What was the point of her life now?

Unbidden came the memory of David's face as she'd looked to him for support. He had let her down exactly when she needed him most. How could he have said he loved her then turned on her like this?

And how was she supposed to face him now?

Only You are faithful, Lord, she prayed. *What is it going to take for me to learn that lesson?*

She wiped her eyes once more. Drew in a deep breath as she looked around. Gained her bearings.

She started up her car and drove back to her apartment. She couldn't go to work today. Couldn't face David after this. Today she was going to be sick. And maybe tomorrow as well. And after that, well, she'd see.

"Any news from Tracy?"

Crystal didn't even look up. "She's not coming in today either."

David leaned back against the counter, his arms folded over his chest. After she'd left social services, Tracy had phoned in sick. She hadn't answered her phone all weekend. Hadn't come to church.

Again and again, like a DVD with a skip, he saw the look of determination on her face when Edgar delivered his ultimatum. She had given it all up for that little boy. Had sacrificed her dream to keep him safe.

Heather had talked about faith, but Tracy lived it.

He felt sick thinking of her betrayed hurt when Danielle and Oden had decided where Kent would go. After Tracy had made her choice in Kent's best interests, she'd still lost.

But what else could they have done? Kent was their first priority, and no matter what Tracy thought of Juanita, Kent and his mother still had a relationship that needed nurturing and encouraging.

"Did she mention when she might be coming back?"

Crystal waved one shoulder in a vague shrug, still not meeting his eye. "She's got a lot of holidays banked up. The girl hardly ever took them. I'd say she's got a break coming."

Since Thursday, Crystal's attitude toward him had been decidedly cool. David had tried to find out what Tracy had told her, but Crystal was also being uncharacteristically guarded. When she spoke to him it was strictly for the purpose of exchange of information.

None of her chatty jokes. No teasing comments.

Dr. Harvey had heard what had happened but hadn't sided with either Crystal or David. In spite of that, work had taken on a gloomy atmosphere. And with Tracy gone, there was an uncertainty in his own personal life he didn't want to contemplate.

He waited a moment, hoping maybe Crystal might volunteer any scrap of information, but she kept her eyes resolutely on the computer screen.

He wanted Tracy back. Wanted to hold her close, to comfort her. To help her through this double loss.

Watch over her, Lord, he prayed as he walked to the

back of the clinic to get his coveralls. *Take care of her. Don't let her keep to herself too long.*

He prayed as he pulled out of the parking lot. Prayed as he drove.

It was all he could do for now.

"He won't move," Emily said, her arms crossed over her chest, her face full of concern as she glanced over her shoulder at Kent hovering by the living-room window, his finger tracing the same circle on the glass again and again. "I told him his mother probably isn't coming, but he won't budge."

"What did she say when she called?"

"She said she was tired. Truthfully, she sounded drunk." Emily drummed her fingers on her arm. "And Danielle called. Told me the police tracked down his mother's assailant. Turned out it was 'Uncle Steve,' the man who claims to be Kent's father. Edgar Stinson's son."

"I guess that's a positive. Juanita won't have to worry about him."

"For now."

David sighed, his heart aching for the little boy. All day his thoughts had alternately jumped from Kent to Tracy. Tracy he could do nothing about except pray and hold down the panicky feeling that she wasn't lost to him.

He walked into the living room and crouched down beside Kent, gently capturing his hand. "Your mommy isn't coming today, Kent," he said softly.

"Yes, she is. She said she was comin'." Kent jerked his hand free. "She told me. She promised."

"She'll come another day." David wished Kent's mother could see this tiny, broken boy. Realize what she had done to him.

I spent a lot of time alone. Tracy's words slipped into his mind and clung. For a moment he saw a young girl instead of a young boy. Waiting. Watching. And he saw a small picture of what Tracy had had to deal with.

"Today. She said Tuesday. Today it's Tuesday. Today she's comin'."

At a loss, David glanced back at Emily, who shrugged. "Do you want me to get you a chair so you can watch better?" David asked.

"I have a table too," Emily said, snapping her fingers as if something had just occurred to her. "We can set it up and maybe, David, you could play a game with Kent while he waits."

A few moments later they had a table set up in front of the window, Kent perched on a chair facing out and David sitting awkwardly on a kitchen chair beside him, setting up the checker board.

Kent glanced down. "Tracy showed me how to play this." Then he looked up at David, his expression tinged with melancholy. "Is Tracy going to come?"

David wished he could answer him. "She went on a holiday. But she'll be back. And then she'll see you."

"She's not in the hospital, is she?"

David felt a jolt, then shook his head. "No. She's just traveling." Crystal had told him that much at least. Said she'd be back on Wednesday. Tomorrow.

The thought of her sent a mixture of anticipation and

sorrow swirling through him. What would she say when she came back? How would she treat him?

And how could he win back her trust?

It was as if all light had been bleached from her life. Even the weather the past few days mirrored her mood, the sun hiding behind dark, lowering clouds that chased each other across a gray sky.

She had spent the past four days driving in a futile effort to outrun her own pain and loss. But each time she stopped, it caught up to her, laid its barbed hooks into her and clung. Sometimes she cried. Sometimes she talked aloud to God, wondering what she was supposed to figure out, what He was trying to teach her. But mostly she just drove.

She'd put over two thousand kilometers on her new car trying to lose her sorrow in the vast and varying landscape of Alberta. Trying to find some purpose in a life that was suddenly rootless and disoriented.

But as soon as she pulled into the parking stall of her apartment, memories of David, of Kent, of her lost acreage, slipped back, as harsh and painful as when she'd left.

She let herself into her apartment, her hands stiff and chilled from the cool, outside air. Winter was moving inexorably toward Preston. A hard, bitter season.

The phone was ringing as she closed the door behind her. The call display showed her it was Danielle. She wanted to ignore it, stay in the quiet place she had found while she was traveling, but the silence of the past four days had proven too much even for her. So she picked it up.

"Tracy?" A deep sigh. "Oh thank the Lord. I was so worried about you. David said you didn't phone him. Where have you been?"

"Traveling," she said.

"Tracy, I'm heartsick over what happened."

You don't have the first clue what heartsick means, Tracy thought uncharitably. You still have your family. Your future. Your boyfriend.

"Tracy, please talk to me."

Tracy sank down on the floor and fell back against the couch. "I don't know what to say, Dani. You know how badly I wanted to take care of Kent."

"I know, Tracy. You did a good job with him."

"And David…" She choked back an unwelcome sob. "I don't know what to think about David. I feel as though he betrayed me. I told him I loved him. I finally dared to say it, and then this…"

Danielle's silence didn't make her feel better.

"He had input into where Kent was going, didn't he?" Tracy asked, pressing her friend for any scrap of information she could get.

"He suggested that Kent be put into Jack and Emily's home, yes."

Tracy winced. "Why?"

"We had a variety of reasons. Don't blame him entirely."

But she did. She had told David things she had never told anyone else. Had entrusted him with some of her deepest darkest fears. And he had used them against her.

"He's phoned me at least twice a day since you left," Danielle said, "Wondering if you've called. Please don't shut him out. He's a good man, Tracy."

"I'll do what I need to do," Tracy said softly. "I gotta go." And then she hung up. And stared out the window of her one-bedroom apartment at the gray, cloudy day outside.

And the shrill sound of the phone broke the silence of the apartment, again. Heart pounding, she glanced at the name on call display. David?

It was Emily.

She had nothing to say to Emily. She heard her own cheery voice, recorded at a happier time, answer the phone, then a beep. Then Emily's hesitant voice…

"Tracy, I hope you get this message. I was afraid to call you before. It's Kent. He misses you. Last night he cried himself to sleep asking for you…."

The mention of Kent's tears made Tracy grab the phone. "Hello, Emily."

"Thank goodness. Tracy, I'm glad we connected. I know this is asking a lot. I know you really cared for Kent and wanted to take care of him yourself, but would you consider coming? His mother was supposed to come for a visit yesterday, but didn't. He asked me if you were in the hospital like his mother had been. He's so mixed-up now."

Tracy's heart contracted at the thought of Kent comparing her to Juanita Cordell. Thinking that she had abandoned him. She had been selfish, and, it pained her to admit, just like Kent's mother. "Danielle told me I had to give him time to settle in."

"I know, but sometimes it's not a good idea. If it's not too hard for you, can you come?"

She glanced at the clock. It was five o'clock. "Can I come now?"

"That would be great if you could."

Five minutes later Tracy was behind the wheel of her car, heading down the road toward Kolvik. The clouds had finally blown clear and the sun was at her back.

As she pulled into the driveway of Emily and Jack's home, she saw a face in the window of their living room. It ducked out of sight and by the time she was out of the car, Kent was barreling down the driveway, calling out her name. He hurled himself into her arms, clinging to her, crying.

"I thought you were gone," he sobbed, clinging to her. "I thought I wouldn't see you again."

Tracy closed her eyes as she held him close, holding back her own tears. "I'm sorry, Kent," she whispered, inhaling his little-boy scent of warm hair and sweat. She shouldn't have stayed away. She shouldn't have punished Kent for her own pain. "I'll be coming to visit more now."

Kent pulled back and was about to wipe his nose with the heel of his hand.

"Hold on, cowboy," Tracy said catching his hand. "I've got a tissue here somewhere."

Kent sniffed and stood unflinching as Tracy wiped his nose. "My kitty is here now." His dark eyes gazed trustingly up at her as he patiently put up with her fussing. "Dr. David brought him. He came for a visit yesterday."

Just the mention of David's name was like cat's claws in her heart. David, whom she still loved.

"Come and see Emily. She's making good food." Kent tugged on her hand, pulling her toward the house.

Emily's home was as beautiful as she remembered it. The late-afternoon sun shone into the kitchen as if welcoming her. Emily was at the stove, creating succulent smells that made Tracy's mouth water. She realized the last thing she'd eaten was a doughnut that she'd picked up at the Tim Hortons drive-through in Spruce Grove three hours ago.

Emily looked up from the pot she was stirring and gave Tracy a cautious smile. "Hi, there. I'm glad you could come."

It wasn't her fault that Kent had ended up here, Tracy thought, trying valiantly to return her smile as she clung to Kent's hand, claiming her small share of ownership in the boy.

"Thanks for asking me." Tracy glanced down at Kent who was swinging her hand in his. "It's good to see him again."

"Come and see kitty," Kent said, tugging impatiently on her hand. "He's really big."

"You go ahead," Emily said with an indulgent smile for Kent. "He's been waiting to show you since I said you were coming."

Tracy followed Kent down the stairs. He had his own bedroom, she noted with dismay. His own bed. A little desk with a CD player on it. His own cupboard. So much more than she could have given him. Kitty was curled up in a soft bed in one corner of the room, his paws tucked under his chin, his whiskers twitching in a cat dream.

"See. He's sleeping," Kent whispered, hunkering down, stroking his kitten with his finger. "He likes his bed."

"It's a nice bed, Kent." And with some reluctance and not a lot of envy, Tracy glanced over at his wooden bed, decorated with various stickers. "It's almost as nice as your bed."

Kent's face grew serious, his finger still stroking his kitten. "I like my bed at your place. Cozy beside you." He looked up at her, his dark eyes sad. "Can I come and stay with you?"

She shouldn't be feeling as though she'd just won some nebulous contest with Kent as the prize. But his question still made her feel important. Needed.

"This is where you're going to stay for a while, Kent," she said, stroking his hair as she always did. "Until you can go back and stay with your mom. This is a good place, isn't it?"

Kent lifted his skinny shoulders in an exaggerated sigh, his T-shirt lifting up past the waistband of the jeans she had bought him. "I suppose," he said, pushing himself upright. Then he brightened, and caught her hand again, pulling her out of the bedroom. "Emily is making supper. We can go see, 'kay?"

He pulled her upstairs and back to the kitchen. "Are we going to eat?" he asked Emily.

"As soon as I'm done cooking we will." Emily smiled down at the little boy, then looked up at Tracy. "He loves helping me in the kitchen."

"Can I set the table?" Kent asked.

"You go right ahead, my dear." Emily tapped a spoon

on the side of the pot and set it in the sink. "Would you like to stay for supper, Tracy?"

"No. No. I just came to see Kent. I don't want to intrude." She already felt as if she had pushed herself on this family. Supper might be considered overstaying the welcome.

"Please? Can't you stay?" Kent clutched her hand, looking up at her with pleading in his eyes.

"I'd really like it if you could, Tracy." Emily wiped her hands on a towel and took a plastic bowl out of the cupboard. "I could use a little help here."

"Well, if you put it that way."

"I'd put it any way I could, if it would convince you to stick around awhile," Emily said, handing her the bowl and a knife. "I need to talk to you anyway, and the kitchen is a good place to talk."

Tracy took the bowl and the knife. In spite of Emily's light manner, she still felt ill at ease. "What kind of salad do you want me to make?"

"The easiest." Emily pulled open the fridge behind Tracy and laid out some lettuce, tomatoes and assorted other produce in the sink. "A green tossed salad. Put in what you want. I'll make the dressing. Kent, you'll need to get a clean tablecloth from the drying rack in the basement."

"Okeydokey." He spun around and ran out of the kitchen.

"He seems to like it here," Tracy said, glancing sideways at Emily. "It's a good place for him."

Emily sighed lightly, her hands resting on the counter in front of her. "I still feel badly…"

"Please. Don't. I could never give him what you've given him here."

"It's not only that. I feel badly about David as well."

Stillness crept over Tracy. A sense of waiting. She stopped working, the cool water flowing over her hands. "What do you mean?"

"That day you stopped by. It was…well, it was a bit of a hard day for our family. We all loved Heather very much."

"She seemed like a person who was easy to love."

"She was." Emily reached over and turned off the tap. Turned to face Tracy. "When I see how David looks at you, though, I know that he never, ever loved Heather the same way."

Tracy kept her eyes on the glistening lettuce in the sink, as Emily's quiet voice sent joy mingled with regret beating through her. What did David think of her now?

"I have to admit to you, when I saw that…" Emily paused. Released a quick breath. "I was jealous. I wanted to keep David a part of our family. Because I felt that if I lost him, I would lose one more piece of Heather."

Tracy chanced a quick glance at Emily, surprised at the admission. "I'm sorry about your sister," she said. "I shouldn't have come that day. Barging in on your family like that."

"You don't need to be sorry. Nor do you need to be jealous of Heather, though I know I was trying hard to make you feel that way." Emily touched Tracy lightly on the shoulder as if seeking a connection. "I know that David and Heather weren't really engaged." Her lips curved in a wistful smile as her eyes drifted past Tracy's shoulder, looking into the past. "I guess I was hoping that by playing along it might actually happen. That David's love and devotion would miraculously heal my sister and they could have their happily ever after."

Emily blinked, as if coming back to reality.

"David told me about the sacrifice you made for Kent," she continued. "He has nothing but admiration for you. And a whole lot more. I know that he loves you deeply. And though I tried to show you a picture of pure devotion between David and Heather, I want you to look at it a different way. I want you to see a man who knows how to be faithful. Who knows how to stay true. He really misses you, Tracy. I saw him after Heather's death. He was sad. But nothing like he's been the last few days."

Tracy hardly dared to believe what Emily was telling her. Didn't know how to fit these words into the emotional upheaval her life had gone through over the past few days. Thinking of David brought her pain. But listening to Emily kindled a flicker of hope and love.

A man who knows how to be faithful.

The words resonated, grew.

"Thank you for telling me this," Tracy whispered. With trembling hands she turned the water back on and finished washing the vegetables. She needed time and space to absorb what Emily had told her.

Chapter Sixteen

"Tracy, another piece of pie?" Emily asked.

Tracy put her hand over her full stomach. "It was wonderful, but I've had more than enough."

"Max, sit down," Emily said. "We have to have devotions yet."

"I hear a truck." The little boy stood up on his chair, looked out the window behind Tracy, then jumped down from his chair. "Uncle David is here," he yelled, grabbing the sliding door to the patio and yanking it open.

Tracy's heart missed its next beat. Not this soon. She wasn't ready to see David yet. But there was no escape. She was trapped between Harmony and Kent and couldn't leave.

"We had pie for dessert," Max was calling, leaning out the sliding doors.

Out of the corner of her eye Tracy caught a glimpse of a large figure, then the soft rumble of the doors sliding farther open and then, there he was, his presence taking over the room

"Hello everyone."

His quiet voice drew her in. It was as if her gaze had its own will and reluctantly she lifted her head. When their eyes met their connection was as tangible as a touch.

"Hey, Tracy." His quietly spoken greeting held a note of intimacy that called to the lonely part of her life. A part that he had easily taken over.

And in that moment of connection she realized through the pain of seeing him that she still loved him.

"Sit down, David. You're just in time for some pie." Emily pulled another chair from behind her and set it directly across from Tracy.

"Sounds great. I could smell it coming up the walk." He sat down, resting his folded arms on the table in front of him, looking perfectly at ease.

Tracy glanced sidelong at Kent, but he was busy with a little car, pushing it along a fold in the tablecloth. No help there.

"Do anything interesting today?" Jack was asking David.

"Not really. A lot of farmers are out in the fields so that makes the large-animal practice slower." David took a plate from Emily and as he smiled his thanks, Tracy's gaze collided with his.

"And how are you doing, Tracy?" David asked, pitching his voice a little lower, as if drawing her to him.

"I'm okay," she said, her voice noncommital. Emily's words resonated in her mind. *A faithful man. A faithful man.*

She needed time to absorb it all. Needed time to pray. To find God first and seek his will. But she wasn't going to get it.

"Now who's here?" Emily said, pushing herself away from the table, looking out the window.

The children, instantly curious, half twisted in their chairs or got up to see.

A tall, thin woman came weaving up the stairs of the deck. Her hip-hugging blue jeans clung to her legs, exposing an expanse of belly that made Tracy shiver. The woman tugged a bright-pink T-shirt down over her navel ring and ran her fingers through stringy brown hair.

"Juanita," Emily said with a light sigh, even as Kent jumped up from his chair, calling his mother's name.

Juanita frowned, cupped her hands around her face and pressed it against the window. Then she smiled a loopy smile and tried to pull open the door.

"Mommy. Mommy. It's my mommy," Kent said, fairly dancing beside his chair in excitement as Emily slid the door open.

Disgust slivered through Tracy as Juanita almost fell into the house, her glassy and unfocused eyes flipping around the room and finally resting on Kent.

"Hey, little boy," Juanita said, holding her arms out to Kent. Kent threw his arms around her and she winced. "I missed you."

Only then did Tracy see the yellow and blue bruise on her cheek, the stitches on her forehead, the fading marks on her bare arms.

"Are you okay, Juanita?" Emily asked.

Juanita looked up at Emily and gave her a sappy

grin. "Well, yeah. You've got my kid. Those painkillers make me feel like I been hit by a lousy gravel truck and my driver didn't come. So I couldn't visit my boy. Oh, yeah. I'm just okeydokey." She grinned again, her attitude at odds with the sarcasm in her voice.

For a split second Tracy could empathize with Juanita. She too, felt as though Emily had "her kid."

"The driver didn't come?" Emily asked. "She told me that she went to pick you up and you weren't there."

Juanita sighed loudly. "I *told* her where I was. She was supposed to get me from there. And she didn't." She shook her head. "Lousy drivers. Couldn't find their way out of a parking lot."

"How did you get here?"

Juanita held up her thumb. "Year-round pass," she said, then reached out for Kent, wrapping one arm possessively around him. "Now I'm here. And I wanna visit my boy."

Emily glanced back at Jack, who had also gotten to his feet. "Kids, we're done here," Jack said. "Max, Rachel, you clear the table. Harmony, you help me load up the dishwasher."

"Why don't we go sit outside?" Emily suggested, putting her arm around Juanita's shoulders and escorting her to the French doors.

Tracy watched Kent skip alongside his mother, swinging her hand. Her mind sifted back and she saw herself, on her mother's good days, walking beside her, looking up at her with the same hope and love Kent showed now to Juanita.

Tracy couldn't help a twinge of envy mixed with

guilt at how gentle Emily was with Juanita. There was no way she'd be able to be as patient with the woman.

Which was probably why Kent had ended up here.

The realization thrummed through Tracy with the accuracy of a well-shot arrow, and, as it did, she looked up at David again.

He was still watching her, his pie untouched. "May I talk to you?"

She couldn't avoid him forever. Tomorrow she'd be seeing him at work. They had things to clear up. She nodded, pushed her chair back and stepped away from the table.

The kitchen was a cacophony of dishes clanging, cutlery being dropped, a few reprimands and a few objections.

David got up, angling his head out the door. "Let's go out on the deck. It will be a little quieter there."

She followed him outside, and they walked to the farthest corner of the deck where they sat down on the sunwarmed bench that lined the railing. Emily and Jack had a large, pie-shaped lot and she, Juanita and Kent had gone to the farthest back corner. She could hear the faint murmur of conversation. Emily had a gentle smile on her face.

"She's a good person," Tracy said quietly, though stifling a momentary flash of envy. "I can see that she's good for Kent and his mother."

"She is good. She's done this lots before." David, to her discomfort, sat down right beside her instead of in the deck chair that was a few feet away. He touched her shoulder and she bit her lip against her reaction, then pulled farther away. "Tracy, I am sorry about how things went. I want you to know that."

Tracy pulled her arms tight against her. Her emotions were too tender yet for his attempt at reconciliation. She felt as if she had been caught in an undertow, twisted around and thrown. She didn't know which way was up anymore. She had lost too much, and, on top of all that, she didn't know where to put her feelings for David. Where to put the information that Emily had given her.

So she kept her eyes focused on Emily's quiet interaction with Juanita. On Kent's smiling face turned up with hopeful love to his mother, even as every nerve ending was aware of David's solid strength beside her.

"I used to do that too, you know," she said softly. "Look at my mom as though this time it would be different."

"It must have been hard for you."

"Unless you've lived that kind of life, I don't know if you can ever know how hard." She didn't mean to sound so harsh.

"Will you tell me?"

Tracy sighed. "I confessed to you before. And look where it got me." She turned to him, wishing that the sorrow on his face didn't call to her so deeply.

"What do you mean?"

"What I told you about my mother. About wishing she was dead. That's part of the reason Kent didn't come to my house, wasn't it?"

"Tracy, I never said anything about that to anyone." He gave a short laugh. "I don't know why you think that's such a deep, dark secret. You wouldn't be the first to think that way about parents."

Tracy held his gaze. "But I'm sure you never planned it like I have." She took a deep breath. "Each time I hear the command, Honor your father and your mother, alongside Do not kill, I know I'm toast. Because I've not only broken those, I've smashed them. I can't see her as my mother. And I can't honor her. And I can't love her. And what kind of Christian does that make me?"

But David didn't look away. "Someone who lives what they believe. Someone who was willing to put all her dreams and hopes on the line for the sake of a little boy she barely knew." He smiled at her, a careful, tender smile.

His eyes pierced hers with an intensity that she couldn't look away from. As his words settled into her mind, into her soul, she felt a kindling warmth.

"Don't say that, David. I'm not a good person. I see Emily with Kent, and I know that he's in a good place now. Better than I could have given him. You were right to have him come here," she said quietly, glancing back at Emily. Emily had her hand on Juanita's shoulder, her head bent as she was talking.

"Juanita's caseworker had more to do with that decision. Juanita absolutely didn't want you to take care of Kent."

Tracy frowned. "I thought you and Danielle made that decision."

"I had input, but I didn't have that much pull." David sat up, as if something had suddenly occurred to him. "Did you think that I…?" He caught her hands, holding them tightly. "Tracy, I recommended that Kent come here for a lot of reasons. But it wasn't because I thought you were a bad person. You've done wonders for that boy. Given him more love than I'm sure he's had in a long time." He touched her cheek, gently turning her face to his.

The intensity of his gaze underscored his words and as he spoke, Tracy felt one more burden slip off her shoulders.

"I will admit that I considered Emily and Jack's home a better place but not because I thought yours wasn't good," David continued, his hand warm on her cheek. "Yes, your relationship with your mother was a factor. I knew that part of what you felt towards your mother would affect your relationship with Juanita as a foster parent. But there were other reasons too. For now, Juanita is hiding behind her situation. Saying how hard it is as a single mom. And she's right. But if you, as a single woman were to take care of Kent, show her up, she'd be left with no defense at all."

Tracy looked back at Juanita, as if trying to see the situation through the woman's eyes.

Juanita was swiping at her face with the heel of one hand, her other arm wrapped tightly around Kent, who leaned against her, his hand wrapped in hers. Emily handed her a tissue and sat back. As if waiting.

Tracy couldn't stop a faint pang of jealousy at the sight of Kent so easily slipping back into his role with his mother. So easily forgiving her.

Just wait, she thought. She'll mess up again.

The unkind thought rose like a snake to face her and Tracy realized that she didn't want that to happen. She wanted Juanita to succeed. For Kent's sake.

Juanita pulled Kent close and wrapped her arms

around him, much as Tracy had only an hour ago. She rested her chin on his hair and smiled.

But if Emily could help Juanita, if Juanita accepted that, then maybe, just maybe Kent had a chance. And she didn't, there were a few more people who were watching out for Kent.

"What are you thinking?" David asked.

Tracy hugged herself and leaned back against the sun-warmed wood. "Right now, I'm trying not to be jealous of Emily. Of what she can give to Kent and what I can't."

"You gave Kent more than you'll ever realize," David said quietly. "More than I'm sure I'll ever realize."

The note of regret in his voice made her turn to him. "What do you mean?" she asked.

He turned his head to her, his eyes soft now. "When I saw you sitting in the restaurant giving up your dream just for Kent…" He laughed lightly, shaking his head. "You asked what kind of Christian you are? I can tell you. The right kind. You sacrificed what you wanted and dreamed, to keep him safe. I'm humbled by what you've done. You've shown me faith in action, Tracy. A faith that doesn't talk but does. A faith I wish I had. That's what kind of Christian you are."

Tracy held his gaze. Saw the sincerity in it. "I don't deserve your kind words. What I did was for Kent…" She shrugged. In spite of her self-deprecating words she felt her cheeks grow warm with his praise. "Anyone would have done the same."

"Not anyone, Tracy. I don't know if I would have had the courage." He sat up. Reached over and gently pulled the collar of her sweater straight, smoothing it with his finger. "You're an amazing person, Tracy Harris. And I'm hoping that the same heart that gave so much to Kent, has a little bit of space left for me. Because you're in mine. I love you."

Tracy closed her eyes, as if capturing his words.

"I know I've made mistakes and I'm sorry for that. I paid too much attention to your mother and not enough to you." He unfolded the collar of her sweater, his fingers lightly brushing her neck. "I was thinking too much about my own brother's regrets, filtering too much of your life through mine." He covered her hand with his. "I want to know what your life was like, Tracy. I want to know because when I see you I see a woman who isn't scared to live what she believes. You're an example to me. I want to hear what you have to say."

She smiled then. Turned to him. "Do you have an hour?"

"For you? I have all the time you need."

"Let's go for a walk."

Chapter Seventeen

She walked with her arms folded, her face forward. But the wary look had gone from her face.

Baby steps, he reminded himself, trying not to panic. She was still talking to him. She hadn't run away.

When Emily had phoned to tell him she was here, he couldn't come fast enough, hoping, praying she would still be here when he came. And she was. And she hadn't run away from him yet.

They rounded the block and she crossed the street to the park she had gone to the day of her mother's aborted visit. He wondered if her mother had tried to contact her at all.

She walked to the same bench, sat down and pulled her knees up to her chest in a defensive posture. She rested her chin on her knees and stared over the playground, now empty of children. Most of them were at home, David suspected, eating supper. Safe in their own places, their own homes.

"What was your life with your mother like, Tracy? I said I'd listen."

She blinked, feathered her hair back from her face with her fingertips. "You want to know what it's like to be the child of an alcoholic?" she asked softly.

"Why don't you tell me?"

She drew in a slow breath as she lowered her feet to the ground, anchored her hands under her knees and leaned forward, as if looking into her past. He took a chance and laid his hand on her shoulders, stroking in small, healing circles, drawing the evil from her.

She gave him a careful smile, then looked away again.

"Imagine you are Kent, sitting alone in an empty apartment," she said, her voice so quiet he had to strain to hear. "It's starting to get dark outside. Getting close to supper. And you're all alone. You hear a footstep. You start to relax. It's okay. Here she comes. Mom is home. And then it goes right on past and your stomach gets a little tighter. It's getting darker, but you don't dare turn on the lights, because then you can't see out the windows anymore. And when that happens, the apartment suddenly becomes even smaller, the windows huge dark expanses that can suck you in. Your stomach is growling. All you've had to eat was a sandwich that a friend gave you. There's not a lot of food in the house this week. Mom forgot to buy it. Again. Lots of liquor, which you've learned to associate with fear and uncertainty, with a mother who turns into a shrill and angry stranger who brings other cold-faced strangers into your home and brings in the rank smell of fear and danger." Her voice hitched.

David felt his own heart stutter in sympathy. He pulled her close to his side and was grateful that she allowed it.

"Pretty soon you get tired of being afraid," she continued, keeping her eyes fixed straight ahead. "And then, one day you venture outside, because that can't be scarier than sitting around waiting for a mother who warned you, on pain of death, not to leave. You meet other people. Get pulled into a circle of friends. You get to know them. And sometimes you stay at their home where it's warm and fun and light. And a mother comes and tucks you in at night. And makes you feel safe. You're in a home where there are two parents standing guard against evil and loneliness. This is a good thing, a bright spot in your life. But the only problem with light is the contrast it creates. Your own place suddenly becomes even colder. Even darker. But once in awhile your mother comes home sober. Sometimes there's supper on the table. Sometimes she plays games and hugs you and makes you feel like you're the most important person in the world. And you dare to think that this time it's going to be better. That you're starting a journey to a good place. But then, a month later, sometimes only a couple of weeks, sometimes a few days, you're sitting alone in the apartment again. Oh, she's full of promises that she will change. She hugs and kisses and cries, and each time her remorse pulls you along." Tracy stopped, took a long slow breath and turned to David, looking him straight in the eye. "And it pulls you along because you want so badly to believe her. Even more than she wants to herself. Because in spite of your fear and your anger and your pain, you still love her. That love is like a hook in your flesh you can't get rid of, and each time it pulls, it hurts."

David didn't look away from the pain in her eyes, or the sorrow in her voice. Because of what he'd seen for only that small moment with Kent, he understood a tiny part of what she'd had to live with. In spite of his own shame, his patronizing attitude, he faced it head-on. He cupped his hands over her shoulders.

"I wish I could take it away for you," he said, his fingers pressing deep into her skin as if he could squeeze the pain out of her life. "I wish I could take it on."

Her gentle smile held a note of melancholy. "Thanks for saying that, David. But Jesus did that already. And that's also been my struggle. To recognize His love and His caring as a constant in my life that has never changed."

"But it still hurts."

She looked down at her intertwined fingers. "Yes. At times, it still hurts. And that's the part I struggle with the most. That she can cause this pain in my life."

"Why didn't you tell me before?"

"I never told anyone before."

"Why not?"

She looked up at him. "Because nobody listened. Not like you're listening now. Mostly they believed my mother."

"I did that too. And I'm so sorry."

Her wistful smile absolved him. Just.

David drew her gently close. Held her against him. "I love you, Tracy Harris. I want you to give me another chance."

She rested her head against his neck, and when she slipped her arms around him, the breath he'd been holding sifted out of him in a sigh. "How can I not?" she said. "I tried to run away from you. Tried to run away from what had happened. But I had to come back here and face it eventually."

"I'm sorry about Kent, Tracy."

She shook her head. "Don't. Please. Don't. He's in a good place. I could never give him what Emily and Jack can. He needs his mother. And Emily can help both of them." She drew away just enough to look up into his eyes. "Which makes me wonder what life with my mother would have been like if I had kept trying to tell someone what I had to live with. If there had been someone like Emily who could have shown my mother how a real mother behaves."

"I shouldn't have pushed you about your mother. I didn't know. Please, forgive me."

"No, you didn't know. But at the same time, you were right. I wanted my mother. There's probably always going to be a part of me that wants a relationship with her." She paused, fingering a button on his shirt. "I didn't dare let her back into my life because I didn't have anyone to fall back on if she let me down again."

David stroked her face with his fingers, sorrow piercing his heart. Sorrow and hope. "For what it's worth, Tracy. You have me. I haven't been as understanding as I could or should have been, but I want you to know I'm here for you. I will love you. As long as you need or want me."

A smile crept over her finely shaped mouth. "Emily

told me that you were a faithful person. That I could trust you."

David felt a rush of gratitude toward Emily. "I hope you will. I hope you'll trust me with your love. And with your life."

Her lips trembled. But only for a moment. Only until she reached up and pressed her lips to his. "I will, David," she whispered against his mouth. "With all my heart, I'll trust you. And love you."

David closed his eyes and held her close. And closer. And sealed their future with another kiss.

Epilogue

"I'm nervous." Velma drew in a long shaky breath.

"You'll be fine. Just don't expect wonders," Emily said quietly.

"But you said she's a good girl."

"She's not a girl. She's a woman who has dealt with a lot in her life and has come out stronger for it. She's her own person."

"She doesn't need me."

"I think she does. You just have to show her that you're worth needing. Show her you can be trusted. But that will take time." Emily straightened, listening. "Here they are."

The sliding doors opened with a muted rumble. "Hello," David called out. "Anyone home?"

Emily got up from the couch in the living room and gave Velma a quick wink. "Here. In the living room."

Velma smoothed her hands over her skirt but stayed where she was, her back to the kitchen, looking out the window onto the snow-covered yard. She shivered, waiting.

"Tracy, you're looking marvelous," Emily said. "Hey. Let me see your ring." Emily sighed. "It's gorgeous. Did you really pick that out yourself, David?"

"I had some heavy hints dropped at my feet by way of catalogs with pages folded over. I can be taught."

"He's definitely a keeper," Tracy said with a husky laugh.

Velma swallowed, then, slowly, got up and turned to face her daughter. She had to do this, no matter what happened.

Tracy's bright smile accented the happiness that glowed from her face. David had his arm around her and when Velma came around the couch, she saw him look up at her then tighten his grip on Tracy. Hold her even closer.

"Hello, Tracy," Velma said quietly. "I heard you got engaged."

Tracy leaned into David, and, for a moment, Velma thought she might not even acknowledge her. Then she nodded. "Just a couple of days ago," Tracy said.

"Congratulations. I heard he's a good man."

"And Tracy is a wonderful woman," David said, caution in his voice.

"I know that. I think I've always known that," Velma said quietly. She swallowed. *God grant me the serenity to accept the things I cannot change...Accepting hardship as the pathway to peace...He will make all things right if I surrender to His will...* "I have to tell you, Tracy. I'm sorry for leaving you alone. For making you scared. For being a lousy mother."

"Why are you telling me this?" Tracy asked. It wasn't hard to hear the pain in her voice, or the mistrust.

"Not for me, Tracy. I'm telling you 'cause you need to know. 'Cause I want to try to be a better mom. And I'm trying to start by letting you know that I know I wasn't always a good mom. And I'm sorry. For you. I'm sorry."

There. She'd said it. Not exactly the way she had written it down. But it was out.

Tracy looked up at David. He smiled down at her. Kissed her gently on her forehead, then together they walked toward Velma. Stopped right in front of her.

Tracy's mouth was quivering. "Thanks for that, Mom," she said softly. "It's a good place to start."

"I want you to forgive me," Velma said. "I can keep going, if I know you forgive me."

Tracy clung to David's hand. "I have been forgiven so much. I've been given even more." She nodded. "Yes, Mom. I forgive you."

Tracy lifted her face as fat, wet snowflakes kissed her warm cheeks. David stood behind her, his arms wrapped protectively around her waist. It was done.

"How are you doing?" he murmured, his voice a gentle rumble in her ear.

"I'm fine," she said, closing her eyes, surrounded by warmth and love.

"Your mother was smiling when we left."

"That's good." Tracy turned and looked up at her future husband, love shining from her eyes as she cupped his face in her hands. "I'm glad you convinced me to try again. I couldn't have done it without you and Emily."

David brushed away the snowflakes clinging to her face, his eyes following the motions of his fingers. "I think you could have. You have a strength that amazes me, Tracy."

"I'm not that strong. I was glad to have you beside me. Holding me."

David kissed her mouth. Then her cheeks. "You are a wonder to me, Tracy."

She stroked his cheeks as she sent up a prayer of thanks. "No, David. I'm not a wonder, you are. You've stilled the voices in my soul. The angry voices that always cried unworthy and unfair. You've shown me that love can be a silence in the heart."

He kissed her again, and arm in arm they walked to his truck.

* * * * *

Dear Reader,

In our role as foster parents, my husband and I and our children got to meet a variety of people and be exposed to a variety of problems. We learned to appreciate our families and to be thankful for parents who care.

In *A Silence in the Heart*, I wanted to show the consequences of decisions that are made by some parents and how it can hurt a child for a long time. At the same time, I wanted to show something that we learned again and again: the love of a child for his or her parent is a potent force and is not easily quenched in spite of the pain that some parents inflict on their children. It is also a trust that can be bruised and bent, a gift that should not be taken lightly.

I want to pray for those families who still hurt, and seek and struggle. For children separated from their parents and the parents who want to change. May God bring people in your life who can help and guide you along this journey.

I love to hear from my readers. You can write to me at Carolyne Aarsen, Box 114, Neerlandia, Alberta, T0G 1R0. Or you can send an e-mail to caarsen@telusplanet.net. Please put *A Silence in the Heart* in the subject line so I know it's a fan letter and not spam.

Carolyne Aarsen

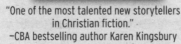

Take 2 inspirational love stories FREE!

PLUS get a FREE surprise gift!

Mail to Steeple Hill Reader Service™

In U.S.	In Canada
3010 Walden Ave.	P.O. Box 609
P.O. Box 1867	Fort Erie, Ontario
Buffalo, NY 14240-1867	L2A 5X3

YES! Please send me 2 free Love Inspired® novels and my free surprise gift. After receiving them, if I don't wish to receive anymore, I can return the shipping statement marked cancel. If I don't cancel, I will receive 4 brand-new novels every month, before they're available in stores! Bill me at the low price of $4.24 each in the U.S. and $4.74 each in Canada, plus 25¢ shipping and handling and applicable sales tax, if any*. That's the complete price and a savings of over 10% off the cover prices—quite a bargain! I understand that accepting the books and gift places me under no obligation ever to buy any books. I can always return a shipment and cancel at any time. Even if I never buy another book from Steeple Hill, the 2 free books and the surprise gift are mine to keep forever.

113 IDN DZ9M
313 IDN DZ9N

Name _____ (PLEASE PRINT)

Address _____ Apt. No. _____

City _____ State/Prov. _____ Zip/Postal Code _____

Not valid to current Love Inspired® subscribers.

Want to try two free books from another series?
Call 1-800-873-8635 or visit www.morefreebooks.com.

* Terms and prices are subject to change without notice. Sales tax applicable in New York. Canadian residents will be charged applicable provincial taxes and GST. All orders subject to approval. Offer limited to one per household.

® are registered trademarks owned and used by the trademark owner and or its licensee.

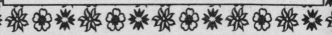